The Rivers of Heaven

ANTHONY GARDNER is a freelance writer and editor of *RSL*, the magazine of the Royal Society of Literature. Born in Dublin, he was brought up in Tipperary and London, where he lives with his wife and stepson. He was previously deputy editor of *Harpers & Queen*.

LUKE ELWES's 'Mustang 1' provides the cover image for this book. His work can be viewed at www.lukeelwes.com.

THE **RIVERS** OF **HEAVEN**

by

Anthony Gardner

In memory of Meryl Gardner

1931-2006

ISBN 0-936315-29-6

STARHAVEN, 42 Frognal, London NW3 6AG
in U.S., c/o Box 2573, La Jolla, CA 92038
books@starhaven.org.uk
www.starhaven.org.uk

Typeset in Plantin by John Mallinson

Happy those early days, when I
Shined in my angel-infancy!
Before I understood this place
Appointed for my second race,
Or taught my soul to fancy aught
But a white celestial thought...
Some men a forward motion love,
But I by backward steps would move...

Henry Vaughan, *The Retreat*

1.

The rivers of heaven surge through infinity: they tumble with the joy of their own being.

Exploding at sheer waterfalls, they project sheer energy – washers of boulders, scourers of stones, polishers of rough, bright pebbles. There is nothing to match their brave exhilaration – the intoxication of their wild, perpetual dance. They hurl themselves from headlong height to chasm, leaping free of time-worn courses, clutching at air; free-falling and cascading and colliding, burrowing into unfathomable pools; flexing themselves and tossing up waves, as quick as youth and clear as autumn sunlight; throwing out momentary fingers of foam that fall and swirl and slalom away.

Everything has urgency – even the sodden, dripping weed – as if there were no eternity, here where all is eternal. But the urgency is soothing: the stones are sluiced and nourished and caressed; they acquiesce to the workings of waters, becoming ever more a part of them. And the waters somersault towards the ocean, answering its cry.

For the rivers are like generals that direct the flow of peace, sending forth the weight of their armies. See how they seem to pause, held in equipoise. Tension breaks, and they tear down from the heights. Flanking major obstacles, they regroup and sweep on; catching their breath in peripheral pools, they hurtle forward again, sparkling, swaying, jostling, giddying the watching eye. Bubbles pushed beneath the surface soar to it again. The waters fold layer into layer, as a peacock's feathers fold.

Brown and green are the colours of the rivers – dull earth hues which the waters bring to life. Matted grass is wedged between stones; ferns and branches reach towards each other. The clumps of moss are like small, drenched animals. Weeds drift like trout, and trout lie in the shallows undisturbed.

All is variation and variegation: stones speckled as snakeskin or bleached with blotches of lichen. (They gleam with veins of gold, all beautiful, precious, here where all is precious and beautiful.) The waters are full of light, like a turned diamond, and not merely with sun refracting through them: they are bright with the light within. Even the sands dazzle. Bubbles rise clearly in the darkest pools, and everything is enhanced instead of muted.

But there are shadows too, cooler, more mysterious than any shadows on earth. They thrill through the light like a low whistle, giving resonance and radiance. Kaleidoscopic, the surface glimmers. At times it even seems to flow backwards.

Less broad than the widest of the earth's rivers, these have a concentrated power, their identity undissipated. Their sense of movement persists, unrestricted by locks or dams. Meanders and ox-bow lakes are not found. The smaller channels and tributary streams are equally industrious in their ways. Observe the eddies at the feet of the bulrushes, the twigs that mimic weighty branches, the small stones thrust up in place of boulders. The water slaps across the ledge of their rapids. It flattens into thinness, plummeting into a trough.

Listen to the rhythmical splashing of water against stone; listen to the splatter of spray on gravel; listen to the gurgle of a sudden hollow. These are the hymns of the rivers, sounds of water near and far adding multitudinous voices to the greater music which pervades the air. It is a music which never cloys, like a favourite song heard as if for the first time, at once familiar and new – like the motion of the rivers themselves, changing as they run, full of comforting repetition but never quite the same, changing as a pebble slips or a shadow shifts or a leaf whirls away on a wave.

He could gaze for ever at the rivers of heaven. But then, he thinks, heaven is like that: every tree, every cloud, every rock deserves unending study. You can loiter if you like, because here is time enough for everything. Time's layers fold together as the waters (as the peacock's feathers) do, and you are worshipping while you are creating while you are watching the rivers churn and hurtle and dash. There is nothing that you would rather be doing, here where duty and delight merge.

But now he is drawn to the rivers as never before – to this river, the strongest and deepest. Its voices call to him, its waves summon, its movements mesmerise. He is walking beside it, gazing at its turbulence and the foam which catapults across its surface. The waters are strong and challenging, suddenly changing pace, appearing to slacken, then whipping away again, moving with the mastery of their art. They lead him to a pool.

2

It is a deep pool, so deep that – even through water which is liquid light – he cannot see the bottom. Two boulders jut by the side of it, adjacent to one another: one as white and dry as desert bone, the other dark with soaking and slippery with weed. Overhead, a branch thrusts out its leaves into sunlight. He climbs on to the dry rock and stares into the depths, knowing the time has come to plunge.

The water is warm, and he can breathe in it. He kicks with both legs, drags the liquid with his arms, propels himself down into silence, his eyes intent on the light. There is nothing else to be seen here: no pebble-strewn riverbed, no flitting minnows, no darting kingfisher – just this embracing abstract, this bubbled greenness. But with every stroke the light becomes fainter, becomes darkness; and his ears begin to fill with dull sound. The water is so thick that he can barely move his limbs, yet nothing pulls him back to the surface. He has entered some kind of tunnel and drifts downwards, forsaking motion, breathing more slowly.

'I am exhausted,' he tells himself. 'I must sleep.' So he draws himself into a ball, sinking ever more slowly towards the source of the sound. It pulses like his heartbeat. He has lost the will to move and feels himself enclosed, as if the walls of a cave had been drawn in around him.

In the warm, heavy darkness he waits.

'Push!' insisted the midwife, and Stella pushed again, bewildered by the pain, baffled by the unfamiliar motion of her body; baffled too that everyone should look to her when the whole situation seemed to have its impetus elsewhere. Her mind called up the titanic corridors of the hospital, the high arches (higher when stared at from the pillow of a trundled trolley), the nurses beside her intent on her spasms, and people beyond – people hurrying along the tramlines of different worlds.

White sheets... symbol of calm, care, competence; now they seemed like the cliffs of a shore left behind. She saw herself adrift on the bed, lapped by waves of agony, with doctors and nurses swimming beside her like tritons and nymphs on the tiled walls of the echoing municipal baths where her grandmother had taken her as a child. She was helpless, humiliated, with – 'No!' she cried as the pain wrenched her again – the secret core of her body exposed to these strangers (but who cared?) – 'No!' again – Who cared? She cared, her swollen, hijacked stomach heaving in the air, struggling to give up its burden.

She wanted peace.

Before all this… there was a place called normality, where her body was her own; and she needed to be there again, feeling smooth and sweet-smelling as a girl straight from her bath, pulling a towel unthinkingly across her waist. ('Push!' *'No!'* It was not a refusal, just the one word she could find beyond a cry – and it seemed worth holding on to.) Let me be that girl, she thought; let me be a virgin, unkissed, untorn, neither wife – not that she was that really, just in common law ('common whore' her mother had said) – nor prospective mother.

But there was no going back. Perhaps she *was* holding back, as the midwife's admonition suggested, trying subconsciously despite blinding pain to delay the moment of motherhood with its concomitant responsibilities, its pram-wheeling captivity. Did she really want this child? ('Come on, love, you can do better than that! Push!')

Of course she did.

She had dreamed of it, prayed for it, long before she had met its father; and when she had seen him for the first time, standing by the pool table in the pub in his tight jeans and white T-shirt, his beautiful hands twirling his cue like Fred Astaire's cane, she had known in an instant that this was the man she wanted to assist her in the act of creation. But Ken had lacked enthusiasm for the role, hungering for the act but not its consequences; he had made himself master of her body, drugging her with sex until she had all but renounced her dream, and she no longer dared try to cajole him into giving his assent.

'No!'

She must want this child, and want it desperately: otherwise she would never have plucked up the courage to defy him, and abandon the Pill, and conceal her pregnancy as long as possible for fear of being forced into an abortion. Occasionally she had allowed herself a fantasy in which he had opened his deep brown eyes in wonder and taken her in his arms, then knelt down and put his ear to her womb, searching for a tiny heartbeat; but instead, predictably, he had beaten her up, blacking an eye and breaking a tooth, before throwing his clothes into a suitcase and going off (she eventually learned) to join the Army. That was why she found herself alone now, at the most crucial moment in her life. Neither her mother, to whom she hadn't spoken since setting up house with Ken, nor her sister, whom she hadn't seen for years, knew anything of her pregnancy; and the prospect of what lay ahead – which managed to insinuate itself even into this delirium of pain – seemed so exhausting that for a moment she thought she might give up now and die, not getting in anyone's way.

4

But the midwife told her to push, and Stella pushed.

And suddenly a living thing came out of her, still part of her, connected by that cord with the unpronounceable name... And the doctor was lifting it high into the light, like a priest raising the communion cup, while it battled for life as if drowning in air.

It was that picture of the priest that stayed in her mind as she fell into sleep or unconsciousness or some heavy blend of the two; and she scrabbled around to puzzle out why, because the church was not part of her everyday life, but something that belonged to her childhood, as one of the places that her gran had taken her to, like the municipal baths, which sailed back and left her no longer able to sort out the doctors and nurses from nymphs and tritons, until they all disappeared, and she was left floating between the tiled walls of a church, where water had reached the top of the pews and sunlight streamed in through stained-glass windows and cast phantasmagorical patterns upon the shifting surface.

Is it a terrible thing to say that a place can mean more to you than your parents do? Probably; but I'm afraid that was the truth about the cottage. Actually, they shouldn't have been angry about it, because I always found it easiest to love them when I remembered what they were like during our times there, before they began to hate each other and resent me.

The house isn't strictly a cottage – it has two storeys and ceilings too high to knock your head on – but there is a thatched roof and an open fire, and the kitchen floor is paved with flagstones which were perfect for racing my battered Matchbox cars. The ancient beams are pockmarked with the passage of woodworm; the ill-fitting doors are equally heavy and dark.

There was no central heating when we first arrived, so at bedtime Mum would fill a hot-water bottle for me from the black kettle – heavy with lime scale – that rattled its lid on a shiny-topped Aga. I used to put on my pyjamas in front of a single-bar electric fire, then dash to my bed and snuggle down beneath a reassuring weight of blankets. Nothing since has ever felt so secure.

Some friends consider me obsessed by my childhood years, and they may very well be right. But they too are prone to bouts of nostalgia, almost always inspired by their adolescence – something I find truly baffling.

I hated being a teenager. I had no self-confidence, no direction. My only claim to cool was a stereo – a present from my father with which I was thrilled until I discovered that it had belonged to his girlfriend, who no longer needed it because she was moving in.

My parents had been divorced for several years by that point, and I spent my holidays being tossed between them like a live grenade. Luckily my passion for photography was in its first flush, and they soon realised that all they had to do to keep me quiet was furnish me with some rudimentary equipment and a darkroom. Not that they didn't love me – at least, I'm sure my mother did; but she had always been insecure, and in her post-divorce hysteria her first priority was to find a new man to look after her. So I hid myself in what had once been the scullery (lit by a red bulb and hung with strips of negatives like prayer chits in a Buddhist temple), ritually bathing glossy rectangles of paper in shallow dishes of mystic chemicals, wrinkling my nose in delight at the vinegary smell and watching for the moment when my captured images began to swim into view.

I didn't rebel much. I wasn't going to make a nuisance of myself at school, because it represented the only security I knew. Instead, my anger was focused on my cooler contemporaries, with whom I regularly found myself trapped in crepuscular sitting-rooms while they stroked the hair of beautiful girls who laid their heads on their laps, listened to triple albums by Led Zeppelin and occasionally handed me a soggy joint. Hours passed like paupers' children hauling carts of ore through Victorian mines.

Photography came to my rescue. I started taking my camera along, choosing my moment, then triggering the flash, casting the slumped figures into ghostly relief. This often went down badly, and I had to move quickly to avoid getting punched; but it gave me a gratifying sense of power. I only wish I'd thought of it earlier.

That was my experience of the 1970s – so you can understand why the Sixties seem like Elysium. In homage to them, I have spent more afternoons than I care to count in specialist record shops flipping through dog-eared album covers in search of a Dusty Springfield rarity, or trawling the Portobello Road for Mr Fish ties. It may sound hopelessly retrospective, but here is the irony: only in the Sixties can I remember the future being eagerly awaited. Those years entrance me as a thrilling meeting of what was past and passing and to come – like a Phil Spector record with its strong, contemporary melody, a smattering of Fifties sentimentality and production techniques which anticipate the whole stereophonic revolution. If you say, as my father does, that

6

it's impossible to generalise about a whole decade, then I'll be more specific: the time that really excites me is from 1963, when Beatlemania began, to 1967, when the age began to lose direction in a hopeless, druggy haze. Since these happened to be the years of my father's greatest success, he would probably agree.

My father, Anthony Terry, was a talented grammar-school boy who happened to arrive at the Royal College of Art at the same moment as David Hockney. He wasn't one of Hockney's best friends, but he managed to reflect a little of his glory, and for a brief time (about three months, as far as I can make out) he was the *enfant terrible* of the British film industry. It was Andy Warhol who got him interested in film-making; with his help my father got the backing to make *Innuendo*, which was banned for obscenity and made him a hero of the underground movement. I've seen it a couple of times: it looks inescapably dated but has some real originality.

Unfortunately, the ban left him in deep financial trouble. The big studios wouldn't touch him, my mother had given up her modelling career to have me, and when a friend offered him a contract to direct television commercials, my father leapt at it. According to my Uncle Robbie, he saw it as a temporary diversion; but he liked the money and liked being at the centre of a young industry about which the world hadn't yet become cynical. The struggle of putting together a feature film seemed ever less attractive, and before long he was promoting the TV commercial as the crucial form of the age – Pop Art on reels. He was nicknamed the Dream-maker on the strength of the exotic worlds he could sketch in thirty seconds of screen time. If someone murmured 'sell-out', he would simply laugh and wave his cheque book with a Harpo Marx expression on his face.

Bizarrely, my father and uncle were once the best of friends. They met at the Royal College, and hit it off from day one; when Dad married Robbie's sister, the bond seemed sealed for ever. My father isn't a blatant snob, but the idea of allying himself to a minor aristocratic family – however short of cash – must have been appealing. Robbie, meanwhile, was trying to divest himself of ancestral trappings and assuming a cockney accent. They were like two lifts, one on the way up, the other on the way down, pausing at the same floor.

Once, as a teenager, I asked Robbie why they had fallen out, and he became so evasive that I didn't press the point. When I asked my father the same thing, he explained it as a fundamental clash over what they were doing with their art.

'Robbie accused me in a very superior way of squandering my talents,' he said. 'I'd like to know exactly what he's done with his. He could have been the British Warhol – bigger than Hockney, bigger than Peter Blake. But he took too many tabs of acid and missed the magic bus.' I think this is overstating the case: I've seen some of Uncle Robbie's early canvases, and though they're really not bad, they hardly bear comparison with Hockney's. What I do admire about him is the fact that he never gave up. Painting is his life, and nothing could stop him believing that the magic bus might eventually come back.

For a long time, when I thought about my father and my uncle, I couldn't decide which was the more tragic – the one who'd prospered by betraying his talent or the left-over hippy clinging to down-at-heel dreams. Both seemed victims of their era; but then what right had I – a less than successful photographer – to make that kind of judgment?

I'm not saying the Sixties were perfect. But they did have idealism, which for most of my adult life has been in pitifully short supply; and although I've always known I couldn't bring them back, I promised myself when I was ten years old that one day I would live in my parents' cottage again.

2.

Heather-covered in lower reaches, thrown round with a thick cladding of snow up high, the mountains climb far, far above the soar of eagles; and to see their terror and beauty is to know the terror and beauty of God – for they were carved neither by glaciers nor by geological disturbance, but by His hand, to be sculptures in blue air, templates of purity.

In the foothills, melted snow saturates the ground, forming surface streams; the sunlight blazes off it, creating molten gold, running in veins unclenched by dark rock. The heather, always in bloom, is thick and resistant under foot, springing back untamed when you have passed. The snipe and grouse watch from their nests without concern, or whirr boldly above you. Grey boulders rise here and there, offering you rest in the sun – as if your limbs could ever be weary.

There are sheep in the foothills; they bound through heather on hidden paths, sure of foot, vigorous of haunch, shrugging forward with the weight of thick wool. They climb to the clouds and are lost among them, ethereally camouflaged, flaunting pure fleeces; they do not fear the red fox or snow fox, nor is the wolf their enemy.

The sheep taste sweet grass in the wildest corners, and they see dawn on the high slopes: for the firmament holds in simultaneity every gradation of night and day, from bright noon to star-calling twilight to the joyful surge of early sun. And beyond snowline and cloudline, the mountains of heaven raise themselves to unfathomable heights, like radiant pinnacles on the crown of God. The clouds wash their slopes as sea washes a shore – white horses of infinity – and the soul dizzies at the sight, unglimpsed by strong-winged osprey or sure-footed chamois. Only the Sun of suns looks down on the mountains' heads and acknowledges their fealty.

The snow neither falls nor melts on these highest reaches; nor is it remoulded by the wind – for here at the birth of eternity it was fashioned to perfection, to dazzle in mound and hollow and drift, abstraction of whiteness given form by its creator. Such is the brightness harboured in its crystals that human eyes would fail; but the soul can see it... and the soul can hear the music of snow, struck by sunbeams from its brittle surface.

From a taxi, Stella stared up at the monumental grey blocks of the estate on which she lived. Behind them the winter sun, silvered and smudged by thin cloud, seemed to be held fast in a frozen grey lake of sky.

'Look, love, we're home,' she whispered to the shape in her arms; but she felt muscles in her face draw tight as she gazed at the stains on the concrete, and washing spread forlornly across balconies. The balance of her moods had shifted away from the euphoria which had cloaked her at Kit's birth: now, like a weary love affair, his existence was something that consoled rather than strengthened. She had shied away in panic from the realisation that she must leave hospital. There, things had felt safe, with nurses to help and feed you and tell you what to do. Here she could see nothing but struggle.

'Hold on, I'll give you a hand,' said the driver as Stella fumbled around trying to get her possessions out of the cab. Two old women stared at her, nylon headscarves framing hostile eyes. She knew what they were thinking – here's another one who couldn't keep her legs closed. She could almost hear them say it.

'There we go,' said the driver, setting down a British Airways hold-all which had once been Ken's. He was a plump, fatherly man with grey hair and spectacles, and she wished that she had a father like him to look after her now, almost as much as she wished that Kit had a father. 'Do you need a hand inside, or can you manage?'

'I'll be OK, thanks.' Then she remembered about paying him and had to put the baby down on the back seat while she found her purse. Nothing was simple now. 'How much is that?'

'Five fifty. Make it a fiver.'

'You sure?' she asked.

'Yeah, go on.'

'Cheers.' She handed him a wrinkled note which the nurse had given her.

'Ta very much.'

'Cheers. Good luck, love.'

It hadn't been easy, getting ready to come home. She had watched other women moving off with their husbands in a warm, busy cloud of security and love to the family hatchbacks which they'd bought with a baby in mind. Waiting for the birth on her own had not been as sad as that; nor had the complete lack of visitors – though it was a strange enough thought that nobody she knew had yet seen her child.

The nurses had noticed her isolation (probably everyone had, though she hoped that some of the mothers had been too engrossed with the fullness of their own lives). They were nice people, who wanted to show concern by asking her about it but at the same time were afraid of rubbing it in. 'Is there anyone you'd like to telephone?' one of them – the redhead with the Scottish accent – had asked in the end; but Stella could think of no one except her friend Sue from the flats, who was away on holiday. She couldn't believe how the others she'd been close to had gradually vanished from her life over the past couple of years; but Ken hadn't liked them, and they hadn't liked him, and when he'd gone she couldn't bear to have them saying 'I told you so'. As for her mother, she would have to tell her eventually; but at the moment it was too much to think about.

Finally, yesterday, she had rung Sue, hoping that she might have come back early for some reason. But there had been no reply, and so when the nurse had asked whether someone was coming to collect her, she had replied that she thought she'd get a bus, if there was a stop near the hospital.

She had dreaded the response – people interrogating her, asking what she was thinking of, exclaiming that surely there was *someone*; but the nurse made a good show of not being horrified. 'You can't take a newborn baby home on a bus. We'll ring for a taxi for you.'

'I can't afford nothing like that.' There was no point in pretending.

'We'll sort something out.' When the time came she'd slipped £20 into Stella's hand.

They could have taken Kit away from me, Stella thought now. If you can't afford a taxi, they might have said, how can you afford to look after a baby? But they were kind. They had told her that someone would come and visit her to make sure that she was all right and help her to sort out her child benefit.

With Kit in her arms and the holdall over her shoulder, she pushed her way through the door of the Albery block. Jagged graffiti which tenants had long since ceased to read glared from the walls, lapped by a tide of rubbish – leaflets and pages of newspapers and cans and plastic bags and other things that didn't bear inspection. Thank goodness the lift was working. Thank goodness no more of her neighbours were in sight either to comment on or to ignore the small presence she had brought with her.

It came as a shock to see the flat so completely as she had left it. There was no reason, of course, why anything should have changed – it wasn't as if anyone around here could think about having a char to clean up after them; but now that her life was so radically different, it seemed inappropriate that the corner of the rug should be flipped over, and last week's newspaper sitting on the table, and the bathroom cabinet's doors ajar, and – worst of all – a carton of milk still waiting to be put back in the fridge. The air had a desperate chill after several days without heating, and the smell of damp was worse than usual: a discoloured patch in the bathroom seemed to have spread further, though she could have been imagining it.

She switched on the light, which only served to make the place look gloomier, and knelt down to ignite the gas fire. The baby whimpered: soon he would have to be changed or fed, without anyone there to tell her how to do it. First she must make up a bed for him – since she didn't have a cot – in the old pram that Sue had given her.

She sat down on an edge of the settee and stared at flames as they laid claim to the squares on the fire's face, creating a glowing waffle. Now she admitted to herself the vanished hope she had not dared think about: she would open the door to find a stack of lager cans on the table and Ken stretched in front of the television watching snooker, looking up to say, 'All right, love?' It was his absence that made this flat so cold and damp and desperate.

She looked at the baby beside her and started to cry.

In those days my uncle lived on a houseboat. The warm fug of the cabin – part paraffin heater, part tobacco smoke, with a distant scent of chemical loo – was one of the most comforting things imaginable. Through misted windows you could just make out the neighbouring boats, one of which had given shelter to Tom Courtenay in *Otley;* in summer, if the glass had been cleaned, you could see the line of traffic squirming along Chelsea Embankment. I don't think I'd have liked to live on board in winter, but it was the best place to drop in for a cup of tea.

'Listen,' Robbie said to me once, 'think of this place as home. If you've got some lady who wants your attention, just put a "Do not disturb" sign on the door.' That's how generous he is. I took him up on it once, but the girl in question complained of sea-sickness.

Because of the damp, Robbie didn't keep many of his paintings on board – he worked in a freezing studio in Earls Court – but there was always at least one canvas jammed in a corner. At that time he was into visionary landscapes: yellow cliffs and purple oceans and trees that floated in mid-air – the kind of things that would have looked great on Seventies album covers.

For an ageing hippy, he kept the place surprisingly tidy. I think it was partly the nautical thing of having to fit a lot of possessions into a confined space and partly the influence of Sabrina, his recently acquired – and much younger – girlfriend, who yo-yo'd in and out of his life in true hippyish fashion but kept house like a card-carrying member of the middle class.

It wasn't until my early twenties that I got to know my uncle well. He was going through what he described as a 'heavy time': his painting had gone to pieces, and he'd been admitted to a series of rehab clinics. My father forbade me to see him – fearing, I assumed, that I would end up sprinkling cocaine on my cornflakes; but as Dad and I were getting on spectacularly badly, this only acted as an incentive.

I went to visit Robbie at a clinic in the country, where the staff eyed me with suspicion and lectured me on the consequences of trying to smuggle in anything a patient might crave. Fortunately, Robbie didn't ask me to do that – he just seemed really glad to see me; and though I hated the place, I kept going back.

It was the first time in my life I'd felt grown-up. Here I was, suddenly taking responsibility – in however small a way – for someone older than me. When they eventually let him back into the world, he was keen to show his gratitude.

'Listen, Silver Surfer,' he said. (He liked to give people comic-book names.) 'In Anglo-Saxon times they had this really weird system of family ties: if somebody was murdered you'd find his fourteenth cousins queuing up for revenge, unless the killer paid them a certain number of cows. The strongest bond was the one between a man and his sister's son – so that's like you and me. When the Viking hordes come and carry off your camera and lights, you light a beacon and I'll rally a band of volunteers. Or whatever.' My uncle loved strange bits of cultural information.

On the day that this story begins, he greeted me with the news that he'd seen my father the night before.

'Really? Where?'

'At the Arts Club.'

'Did you have dinner with him?'

Robbie laughed. 'No way. He doesn't want to be seen hanging out with an unreconstructed flower child like me. He'd bought some suit with him – said they had business and spirited him across the room before you could say Speedy Gonzalez.'

'Was Vicky there?'

'Skinny bird with a face like an off-colour armadillo?'

'That's it. Hadn't you met her before?'

'Maybe in another life: I think she was a weasel and I was a rabbit. But not this time around. Like, how often do I see your father? Once every two years? Is he serious about this chick?'

'I'm afraid so. She moved in with him three months ago. I don't think she'll stop at anything short of marriage.'

'What is she – an arms dealer? Eco-terrorist?'

'Not quite. She works in the City. Eurobonds or financial futures or something like that.'

'So why isn't she shacking up with some fat-cat stockbroker instead of a has-been adman?'

Just occasionally, Robbie could sound bitter about his old friend.

'Dad's doing OK. Besides, a lot of City people think advertising is very sexy. How's Sabrina?'

'Oh, she's cool. She's gone to the country for a while. She wants to do a book about fungi. I said she should talk to you.'

A lot of people had suggested book projects to me over the years, but as most collapsed after a few meetings, I didn't get too excited about them any more. For some reason on this occasion an extraordinary image flashed into my brain. It was of a ghostly toadstool caught in close-up and almost glowing out of a dark background with a vividness that would haunt me in the weeks and months that followed.

'That sounds really interesting. Tell her I'd be happy to discuss it.'

'That's good. She'll be pleased.' He took another sip of tea.

'So what else has been happening?'

He shrugged. 'I've been working on a couple of canvases' – and he was off, explaining at length the concepts behind them. 'People who knock fantasy always say, "Hey, it's so easy, there aren't any rules." But that's what makes it really difficult. You've got to invent the rules, and stick to them. Art without rules doesn't work.'

'I'd like to see this new stuff.'

'Well, you know, drop by the studio whenever. Only remember to wear your Arctic survival suit. It's chillsville there at the moment.'

'I will,' I said. 'Thanks.'

14

But my mind was still on those mushrooms.

Caught now in this small body, Kit struggles in vain to master his limbs. Legs and arms flop and dangle; his head lurches when it moves, spinning everything past his eyes at giddy, fearful speed. All that he sees is of such vast proportions! It is as if he is gazing at this new world through a massive, rotating magnifying glass or in a distorting mirror from an amusement arcade. He lies in a giant's room, in the soft corner of a couch, and looks dizzily up at acre upon acre of ceiling.

He does not move through this world as he wills; hands lift him, usually gently, and bear him through air. He is learning to relax and accept this, as you accept a dream because you know that it is a dream and that it will eventually set you down on your bed again and steal away. And because he is not yet sure that his life on earth is itself anything but a dream, he is beginning to accept that too. But these hopeless limbs frustrate him, and this mouth that issues only inarticulate wails, and this stomach that demands so tyrannically to be filled that it moves hunger into the realms of pain.

His mother's breast fills his field of vision; his hands reach for it involuntarily, feebly, moving through space as if they were pushing through glue. This is the only stability that he knows now, this purely physical thing, offering warmth and softness and nourishment, and he drinks from it desperately yet distrustfully, like a castaway forced at last to gulp water from the sea, although well aware that it may send him mad. Imperceptibly, his body grows stronger; imperceptibly, his mind becomes less clear. He wonders if the milk is a drug, binding him to this earth.

His mother speaks to him with words that are beneath his understanding, just as his cries are beneath hers. Ears tuned to the music of the spheres cope poorly with this rough language in which phrases are dragged across the airwaves like scrap metal clanking upon tarmac. He does not attempt to understand them, for why learn the language of a country in which you expect your stay to be brief?

He sleeps much, because in sleep he returns to the world from which he has been exiled. In his dreams he moves sure-footedly, treading meadows and forest paths, hearing the ocean's surge and peacock's shriek, encountering in everything a vividness which his life on earth lacks. It is not altogether unreal, his waking life: but he is distanced from it, as if he were remembering its events rather than experiencing them; only when he closes his eyes and basks again in the light of

15

heaven does he recognise actuality. And when he wakes, he cries out not only at the hunger which stabs his stomach, but at the shock of alien surroundings to which consciousness consigns him.

He is grateful to his mother, because she looks after him: he likes her smell, and reads devotion in the enormous eyes that watch him intently. But the emotion he feels towards her cannot be described as love, for it is the product of dependence, not something freely given. He does not understand her role in bringing him to this existence; if he did, he would certainly resent it. He is, in his mind, the offspring of nobody, but of eternity.

Curiously, Stella has something of the same feeling. In spite of the longing and heaviness of pregnancy and agony of birth, she would not claim to have planned this child. He has come to her as a gift, a foster-ling, something for which she takes responsibility but no credit. She called out and was heard; she supplied a vacuum and it was filled. She remembers snatches of a prayer and thinks of herself as a handmaiden, acting out her appointed role. As for Ken, where he fits into this scheme of things she is not sure. She longs for her child to have a father but almost believes that by rejecting responsibility for Kit, he has undone his part in the act of creation.

By assuming the role of priestess, she makes her burden easier to bear. As the vessel of a higher power, she cannot be blamed for the situation in which she finds herself. The instructions which health visitors give her on the care of her child are absorbed like directions for a holy rite; even the act of changing a nappy achieves a kind of sanctity. Her dank, decaying flat is less oppressive as a temple consecrated to Kit's upbringing, with the paraphernalia of babydom laid out in celebration like cards and presents at Christmas time, the odour of baby-wipes substituting for incense. The health visitors, though worried by her exhausted appearance, are impressed by her devotion and eagerness to learn.

So the child grows ever stronger, yet ever more confused by the two worlds between which he passes.

3.

My parents' cottage stands on the edge of a small Cotswold village called Harbury. Everybody has his own dream of England, and Harbury is mine – above all on a summer's day when the dust lies white on the roads and the houses' yellow bricks seem heavy with heat; when the only sound is the rasp of a grasshopper and you walk down the hill beneath a canopy of branches and catch a sudden scent of cool earth drifting on a breeze. Other Cotswold villages of course have these ingredients, but they also have coach parties and tea-rooms selling fudge and antique shops selling pokers and knitwear shops selling knitwear, all of which Harbury has been spared. The sixteenth-century pub, The Goat, attracts a certain number of outsiders, but they tend to hide away in the well-groomed garden at the back. The only person likely to disturb you as you walk between lichened walls is a local jogger with his terrier at his heels.

Here I am, talking like the oldest inhabitant, as if I'd never discovered the taste of exile.

Journeys up to the cottage from London were always an ordeal. First there was the saga of packing my father's Fiat, which was a sporty number with zero luggage capacity; then there was car-sickness, to which I was a martyr, and an inevitable argument about my father's driving. But on arrival at the cottage, everything seemed suddenly all right. 'We're almost there, Sebastian,' my mother would say, turning to me in beautiful silhouette, with a smile I could barely see but could hear in her voice. I would lean forward, thrusting my face between the front seats, cheeks compressed as I strained for a glimpse of the signpost saying 'Harbury' illuminated for an instant by our headlights; my father would change gear as we descended the hill, then bring the car to a halt by our garden gate. I would tumble out, giddy for a moment, and stamp around to regain full use of my legs while Dad unlocked the front door and turned on the lights. To run from room to room was to be an explorer, discovering the cottage as if for the first time.

Unpacking was infinitely preferable to packing – carrying in my suitcase and a box of toys which I emptied on the floor beside my bed. The Aga would be stone cold, but my father would get a fire going in the drawing-room and my mother would fry sausages in a scorched pan while I crouched beside her trying to toast slabs of bread, which fell into the ashes when the heat became too much for me and had to be dusted off. There would be a lot of laughter, and suddenly I could see us sitting there like a happy family in one of Dad's commercials and would believe for a while that that was what we had become.

Behind the house was a large garden and beyond that a field out of bounds to me on my own, since there was a small river running along the bottom of it. On hot summer days we used to go down and swim; at night my parents and their friends would return for skinny-dipping, or at least that's what the people in the village believed. I can't remember any nudity – just girls in kaftans spread out across the lawn like basking butterflies.

I liked these visitors because they were indulgent towards me and undermined my parents' best efforts to send me to bed. I would run among them from high noon until the sky was shot through with stars and the air full of barbecue smells, and someone would play the guitar or tune a transistor-radio to a pirate station. Sometimes complete strangers turned up and stayed for several days.

When I meet friends of my parents now, they still talk about those parties. They give a little laugh and wry smile and shake their heads as if to say 'Wow!', then remember that they're chief executive of ICI or whatever and reach for their mobile phones. My father finds the subject embarrassing – he doesn't like discussing anything that happened when he was married to my mother; but Robbie can occasionally be persuaded to reminisce about the time when he and Jean Shrimpton went picking blackberries by moonlight or George Harrison arrived with Patti Boyd. Perhaps there were awful things too – an ambulance coming for someone who had OD'd, or people getting themselves involved in strange sexual permutations which they afterwards regretted; but if so, I was unaware of them.

Then it all finished. My parents separated; neither took me to the cottage any more. I was sent off to boarding school, aged barely seven, the youngest pupil that Deanswood had ever had. It was not the beginning of the happiest days of my life. It was the end.

The cottage was the one thing – apart from me – that continued to link my parents, because by the time my mother finally agreed to a divorce they had acquired an elderly sitting tenant; the property market had slumped as well, so rather than sell the place they had decided to hang on until the economic situation improved and the tenant dropped dead. He proved a tough old bird though, and when things began to boom again in the mid-Eighties he was still there, as healthy and immovable as ever; which proved beneficial to me, because my parents gradually got used to the idea of doing without the cash, until on one extraordinary day my father promised me that when the cottage at last fell free it would be mine. It was a gesture intended, I think, to clear whatever guilt he had accumulated about me over the years – which was fine by me.

Shortly afterwards I began visiting Harbury every few months to look at my future property. I wasn't sure, to begin with, that it was the right thing to do; but I soon discovered the effect to be therapeutic. It didn't matter that I was excluded by walls that should have hugged me in: this was where I belonged.

The garden was maintained well enough, though I wasn't keen on the hollyhocks which lined up beside the front door like lanky farm hands come for their weekly wages. Mr Czernowsky (a wartime refugee from Poland, I discovered) mowed the lawn by hand, slogged around with a large plastic tank spraying greenfly, and cleaned the windows from an aluminium ladder. One way or another, he seemed to have a lot of life left in him.

I finally met him at The Goat, where I went for lunch on these expeditions. He came in, ordered a pint of bitter and addressed me from the bar.

'You have been watching my house,' he said, in a high-pitched voice rich with Eastern Europeanness. Fortunately there were only two other people there and they were too engrossed in an argument to notice. Still, it was pretty embarrassing.

'It's not your house,' I said. 'It belongs to my parents.'

This must have sounded more aggressive than I intended, because he marched across and glared at me through gold-rimmed glasses.

'I have every right to be there,' he said. 'The law is entirely clear. Continue to harass me, and I will report you to the police.'

'You don't understand,' I said. 'I'm not trying to drive you out. I simply like to come and look at it now and again. I'm sorry if I upset you. Let me pay for your drink.'

'Very well,' he said, and – to my surprise – held out his hand. I passed him a £5 note, which he took to the bar, returning with his pint and the change. Then he sat down opposite me. 'We had better get to know each other.'

He was a small man, with particularly tiny hands and feet; his head was bald, except for a parapet of short grey hair. He wore a black suit, slightly shiny at the elbows, and a Fairisle jersey curved over his little pot belly.

'My name is Tadeusz Czernowsky,' he said. 'But of course, you will already know that.'

He then began to cross-examine me about the basic details of my life – name, age, education, employment, marital status – as if he were interviewing me for a job or weighing up my right to reside in the United Kingdom; I replied, more bemused than irritated, between mouthfuls of cheese sandwich. When he had finished that, he gave me an unprompted run-down on himself – which was not, it has to be said, very exciting. He had served as an RAF mechanic during the War, then worked in a London furniture company, eventually becoming MD. He had always wanted to retire to the country. He had been a widower for twenty years. That, apparently, was it.

It was a novel approach, and not one that would have gone down well on the cocktail-party circuit. Still, there was something to be said for it: one can, after all, spend whole evenings talking to people and miss the one fundamental piece of information that puts everything else in perspective. But I felt glutted with facts and starved of the subtle manoeuvrings that elevate conversation into an art.

Then he asked whether I played chess.

'A little,' I replied. 'At least, I used to at school. I don't suppose I've had a proper game since I was fifteen. I always thought that draughts were rather more fun.'

This was clearly the wrong answer.

'Chess is the greatest intellectual pursuit known to mankind,' he said – rather huffily, I thought. Partly out of mischief, I refused to swallow this.

'It's certainly a very demanding one. But I wouldn't say it's the greatest. What about nuclear physics? Or writing epic verse?'

'No one writes epic verse any more. Nuclear physics is the preserve of a few specialists and will soon be considered old-fashioned. Chess will never be superseded. I have solved problems devised by men long dead, and struggled with others that will tax the minds of generations to come. I have played with a nobleman in the Luxembourg Gardens, and an illiterate seaman at the docks in Algiers. Nothing in life has given me more pleasure.'

'Not even love?'

'Certainly not love. If love was governed by the same hard rules as chess, the world would be a much more agreeable place.'

'But chess doesn't achieve anything. You simply spend hours trying to outwit somebody else. I consider that a waste of mental energy.'

'Of course chess doesn't *achieve* anything, as you put it. That is part of its appeal: it is pure, abstract. But that is not to say that it is pointless. You must be a very hard-working young man if you do not know the value of recreation. What do you achieve when you visit the gymnasium? Nothing tangible; but you are nonetheless doing yourself good. Chess is a whetstone for the wits, a passport to a higher realm. *Mens sana in corpore sano.*'

'Do you play every day?'

He shook his head. 'There is not that opportunity in Harbury. There used to be a fellow here that I played against with some regularity, but he is dead now. Sometimes I go to Oxford to take part in a tournament, but I do not enjoy cities much any more. Most of my games are conducted by post card or telephone; I also have many books of chess problems. But it is not the same as having an opponent in front of you: I miss that. We could have a little game now if you're not in a hurry.'

'If you like,' I said, not because I had any great desire to play but because I was curious to see inside the cottage. To my disappointment, he produced a miniature board from his pocket and laid it on the table between us.

I didn't know quite what to do when he stretched out two clenched fists towards me. I decided that it must be the beginning of a special ritual – like the haka performed by the All Blacks – so I mirrored his gesture. He laughed as if it was the funniest thing he had ever seen.

'In each of these hands,' he explained, 'I have a different-coloured pawn. The one you choose will decide which colour you play with.'

I made my choice, feeling very stupid, and of course picked black. I felt even stupider after the first few moves, when I realised that he had almost got me into a fool's mate. I managed to foil that and held my ground better than I'd hoped; but nevertheless, before The Goat closed for the afternoon I found myself soundly beaten.

'I'm a bit rusty,' I said.

'I don't think that is the problem,' he replied matter-of-factly. 'I think that you simply lack a talent for the game. Even if you played all day every day I doubt that you would be any good.'

I began to feel quite angry. I had had enough of being patronised by this ridiculous old man who was cheating me of my birthright.

'Rubbish,' I said. 'If I had been playing since the Franco-Prussian War like you, you wouldn't have lasted fifteen minutes. It's simply a matter of training your mind.'

Thinking about it now, I can hardly believe that it happened so quickly and so simply; but Czernowsky studied me for a moment with a mixture of amusement and scorn, and then said, 'The day you beat me, my young friend, I will move out of your parents' cottage.'

'Right,' I said. 'You're on.'

As we left the pub, he set his terms.

'You will come to Harbury and play with me for at least four hours a month. If you fail to keep to this arrangement, the wager will be off.'

'If it's a wager,' I said, 'what is there for you to win?'

'Simply the satisfaction of showing the superiority of age to youth. It will reassure me that I am not yet senile. If you start to get the better of me, I will know that I am in an advanced state of decay, and that it is time for me to move into an old people's home.'

So I went off and started to learn about chess.

'Just keep it away from Kit, that's all.'

'God Almighty, listen to her! My own daughter telling me where I'm allowed to smoke my bleeding fags. Excuse *me*, your ladyship! Acting like a bloody school teacher instead of a scrubber with a bastard kid who's no better than she ought to be.'

'Leave it, Mum. I never asked you to come here. If you're staying, I won't have you giving Kit lung cancer, or talking about him like that.'

There is a new person in Kit's life. She is the largest one he has ever seen, with a bosom which threatens to suffocate him, and thick, flabby arms which offer none of the security that his mother's provide. An acrid, dead smell hangs about her clothes. Her hair is bright orange, and she fills half the sofa. When she picks him up, he shrieks to be released.

'So that's the thanks I get for coming all the way to see my grandchild. Ta very much. Your stepfather was dead against it, you know.'

'I know.'

Kit lies quiet. He senses his mother's distress but is too exhausted to cry out on her behalf.

'That Ken ain't been to see him, I suppose.'

Stella hesitates. 'No,' she says at last.

'I knew it. Don't say I never warned you, cos I did.'

'Please Mum, don't.'

'I told you there was only one thing he wanted from you.'

Stella starts to cry. There was certainly only one thing she wanted from him. Love, love, love.

Her mother lights another cigarette. 'Look at this place. I'm surprised those social workers let you keep a kid here. You ain't got no pride, that's your trouble.'

Stella sobs; Kit musters his strength and joins in. His grandmother goes into the kitchen and starts washing up.

When she comes back, the situation is a little calmer. Stella is perched with Kit on her lap, rocking backwards and forwards, waving an ancient teddy bear in front of him. Her mother sits down again on the sofa.

'So what you going to do – sit here on your own with him for the next five years, living on hand-outs from the social security? You'll go barmy.'

'I don't know. Look for a job maybe. Got to, really. Keep my mind off things.'

'Who's going to give you a job?'

'I'll find something. I'll clean. Put an ad in the newsagent's window. Something.'

'God help us. Look at my two daughters: one too la-di-da to speak to us, the other lucky to get a job as a char. And does she take a blind bit of notice of anything I say? Not bleeding likely.'

Kit gazes out of the window. There are clouds in the sky – immense, noble clouds, white against blue, like the clouds of heaven. What brings them here? Why do they pause above the dreary urban landscape? Perhaps they have a message for him; perhaps they are here to take him home again.

His eyes open wider, and his soul rises to join them, boarding these galleons of the air, sensing their restlessness. Massed together, they drive on, spreading outwards in a great mantle; then they cut loose, fragmenting, floating free from one another, only to reassemble and bind and break like before.

Their nomadic ways appeal to Kit. Along the silk roads of air he sees them accelerating towards new hemispheres; he feels the urgent call and surging drive of the wind. When the armada pauses, it is merely visiting a higher harbour, where it can gather strength before weighing anchor and taking a fresher wind, buccaneering out across the thin ocean.

So he flies with them. He climbs aboard and lets their momentum carry him above the land as shadows race behind. He sees a silver-grey river turning ponderously through the city and setting its face to the sea; he watches the coastline fall behind, and then the mass of water mirror and mimic the mass of sky as clouds rush towards a fresh continent. The winds sing around them as Kit gazes down on tracts of heavy, foaming waves pursuing long wanderings of their own. He feels at home with their boundlessness, their aspirations to infinity.

He floats, it seems to him, for days over these seas, over plains and forests and mountains; and when he feels giddied by perpetual motion, he swims up to the surface of clouds, where nothing interrupts the sun, and rejoices in a whiteness that stretches away on every side in dazzling tranquillity. He roams its canyons and rests in its pavilions, until the sun is gone and light thinned out to the very edge of the sky in threads of orange and green and blue.

Then the stars come out. One after another they step into the sky as if for his benefit – like a sky tribe gathering to meet a stranger washed up on their shore – and form their constellations: the bear, the twins, the hunter, the winking crab. And he dances among them, touching their cold fire, tumbling on the broad span of the Milky Way, holding out his hands to catch comets blazing through darkness. He laughs at the radiance of the cratered moon, and Saturn, quaintly ringed, set before him like wondrous cosmic baubles; at his feet is the earth, luminously blue, dusted with the clouds he travelled on, the jewel of creation, revolving with its mighty seas and handsome continents; and all around him the stars are studs in the doors of eternity, guarding unguessed passageways through space and time and stranger dimensions. But he feels no fear in this celestial garden, where suns bloom and fade like flowers against blackness – his heart is filled with the joy of endless possibility, of perpetual change within an ordered frame, of the meeting of actuality and desire. So he sings – or does he mime to a song the planets sing? – and praises his creator, this child of forever.

But then he can no longer sing. There is something that clutches at his stomach: hunger. He is blinded to the stars; loses his footing in the clouds; plummets, gasping, into earthly consciousness, and stretches out his lungs to cry for food.

His mother clasps him to her, but her warmth and love do not suffice to assuage the pain inside. Then the longed-for flow of milk begins,

24

and he sucks for all he is worth, drawing it down into his gut to smother the domineering pangs. But there is no milk for his heart.

'How have I come to this?' he wonders. 'How have I come to this?'

'He's a greedy little beggar,' says his grandmother. 'Just like that no-good father of his.'

'Ask him if he's going to be much longer,' said Andrea Meissen.

'Bitch,' I thought. She was sitting only ten feet away, on a Gothic chair which (in the most ludicrous coals-to-Newcastle exercise) I had almost killed myself transporting from the King's Road to Shepperton Studios. She could perfectly well have addressed the question to me; but since she was – as of three months ago – a semi-famous actress, it was beneath her dignity to talk directly to a photographer.

'I'll find out for you, Miss Meissen,' said Dick Mildmay, standing five feet from each of us and thus ideally placed for bouncing signals off. 'Ah, Sebastian, how long is all this going to take?'

'It'll be over before you know it,' I said with professional evasiveness, flashing a smile at each of them. 'We're almost there with the lighting. Then I'll do a couple of Polaroids and we'll get straight down to business.'

'Ah, not long, Miss Meissen,' said Dick Mildmay with nervous cheeriness, just in case she hadn't heard.

'I'm not hanging around much longer. I want at least half an hour with the masseuse before I go back on set.'

'Don't worry, Miss Meissen, we'll see that you get it.'

It was my first cover shot for *Frontier*, and although ideally I would have spent an afternoon on it, I had reconciled myself to making do with two hours. As it turned out, my subject called a halt with just under half an hour on the clock.

'Do I have final approval on these pictures?' she asked.

'Does Miss Meissen have final approval?'

'I'm afraid that's not up to me,' I said. 'You'll have to speak to the art director.'

'I'll see to it, Miss Meissen.'

I felt sorry for Dick Mildmay. He was a tall, beer-gutted man in his fifties, with a blotchy complexion, crooked teeth and hair that was slipping away as if embarrassed to be party to such a spectacle; the only thing that seemed to be holding him together was his stiff, well-cut pin-stripe suit. His story was written on his face in a cuneiform of broken veins: he had come into the PR business when it was still a new game and had spent his twenties and thirties at four-hour lunches; married a nice Home Counties girl, put three children through public school and spent winter weekends shooting with clients. The dawn of the ruthless Eighties had found him an undiagnosed alcoholic; he had lurched into mid-life crisis, started an affair with an office junior, and in quick succession lost his wife and his job. Now he was reduced to indulging the whims of this apprentice prima donna.

That at least was how I understood the situation. But later, as he and I headed off for a drink in the VIP canteen, I realised that I had underestimated his resilience, and his professionalism.

'Gather ye plaudits while ye may,' he said. 'I give her two years on the verge of stardom, and then it'll be Agatha Christie and game shows for the rest of her days, poor love.' He spoke without viciousness, and I saw that his nervous sycophancy towards his client was not born of desperation but of an instinct that this was simply the best way to handle her. He could have acted her off any stage in the West End.

When our Bloody Marys arrived he asked whether I was related to Anthony Terry.

'He's my father.'

'Is he now? I must say, there is a certain resemblance – but I'm sure you're sick of being told that. What's Tony up to these days?'

I told him.

'I get the impression,' he said, 'that he hasn't exactly cornered the market in filial respect and affection.'

'We've never got on particularly well.'

'That's a shame. I adored my father. I don't quite know what he'd make of me if he saw me now.'

'I've got a pretty good idea of what Dad makes of me. He always said that he wanted me to be a hot-shot adman, but I think he'd probably resent me just as much if I was.'

'So Robbie McLelland is your uncle.'

'That's right. He's great. I'm very fond of him.'

'I used to see quite a lot of both of them in the Sixties. We seemed to go to the same parties. God they were marvellous, those days! The birds! I tell you, if you fancied that girl over there – ' he pointed to a pretty blonde wearing a flapper's costume – 'you'd chat her up, take her out to your car, wham bam thank you ma'am, and then go off and meet your girlfriend for dinner. That's how laid-back we all were.'

A lot of people find this kind of reminiscing deadly dull, but not me. I sat mesmerised as he told me about some of the people he'd worked with – Honor Blackman, Sandie Shaw, Terence Stamp. That carried us into our third round of Bloody Marys, and I began to feel quite drunk, though the alcohol had no discernible effect on him.

'The thing is,' he said, 'if anyone had asked me in those days who was going to make it really big, I would have said your uncle, without a shadow of a doubt. He was one of those people who had everything going for him: the birds adored him – he was very handsome in a Scott Walker-ish sort of way – and he came from a very good family, though he did his best to cover that up, and he was an extremely promising painter. Your father, I'm afraid, always seemed a bit of a plodder by comparison. But then, life's often like that. One moment someone's hanging on in your slipstream, and then suddenly – whoosh! – you can't see their arse for dust. I suppose it was the Warhol connection that did it for your father. Your uncle just hung around with things never quite happening until he gradually vanished from sight. What's happened to that glorious mother of yours, by the way?'

'She's living in Turkey.'

'Good Lord. What's she doing there?'

'She's got a house near Bodrum. She moved there about five years ago. She runs some kind of shop selling things to tourists.'

'You haven't been out to see her?'

'I almost went a couple of years ago, but then she said it wasn't a very convenient moment, so I called it off. It's time I made another effort, though.' I didn't tell him what I suspected to be the real situation, which was that Mum had set up house with some man who was rather younger than her and was embarrassed by the idea of having her grown-up son hanging around.

'Come to think of it, I heard something about your father the other day – that he was going out with Vicky David. Is that right?'

'Yes. Do you know her?'

'I do, unfortunately. A friend of mine in the City got tangled up with her; almost married her, in fact.'

'Why didn't he?'

'She dumped him. Apparently she discovered that he was earning less money than she was, and she had made a solemn vow never to go out with anyone poorer than her, because she couldn't respect him.'

I said nothing.

'Whoops,' he said, 'I can see I've spoken out of turn. Sorry. You're probably devoted to her and wish it was you she fancied instead of your father.'

I laughed. 'No thanks. I was just trying to imagine what it would be like to have her as a stepmother. Pretty frightful, I'm afraid.'

'Well, for your sake I hope it never comes to that; and if it does, watch your back. I've seen my share of women like that, and believe me, they stop at nothing. I'd rather marry a crocodile with a cocaine habit.'

'I'd better go,' I said. 'I have to get this film developed tonight.'

'And I have a dinner to go to.' He pushed back his chair and got to his feet.

'By the way,' I said as we walked towards the exit, 'do you happen to play chess?'

Stella wheels Kit through the supermarket. Gazing up, he moves past forms whose like he has never seen before: old, stooped people labouring along the aisles; brisk women in high heels loading trolleys; children hurtling by, not much higher than himself. He glimpses worry-lined faces and lipstick-smeared mouths, heads of messy hair, grizzled cheeks, bloodshot eyes; he witnesses jostling and impatience. Never before has he been aware that imperfection could exist in such abundance and variety. He looks for beauty and detects only a faint undercurrent. He feels frightened and out of place.

But the shelves of brightly packaged treasures intrigue him. He is transfixed by the huge boxes of detergent, ranks of different-coloured jams, heaps of pale apples, fat plastic bottles of fizzy drink; he reaches for flan cases and dustbin-liners, for canned soups and tubes of toothpaste. Though in themselves they mean nothing to him, his excited mind registers that new discoveries stretch before him as far as the eye can see, here in this strip-lit hall of bounty. Discovery, however, is interspersed with terror as colossal trolleys and swinging baskets of shining mesh sweep threateningly towards him.

His mother pauses for a long time at each stopping point, lifting and examining tins and packets, returning them to the shelf, taking new ones and scrutinising them in their turn. This gives Kit an opportunity to focus on individual objects in the same way. The spice rack intrigues him most.

Then they take their place in a row of people moving towards a beeping till. A strange face dips to admire him; its owner exchanges quiet words with his mother; they laugh. He is wheeled a few steps forward. The cashier looms. Stella places her findings before her; but she has not got enough money. Kit senses her embarrassment and despair.

Chastened, they leave the temple of consumption with what they can afford. Kit looks again at the hanging signs that point the way to frozen food, preserves, the wholegrain bakery, household goods; he sees blazoned offers, only £1.89s, special displays, holiday-for-two-in-the-Caribbean leaflets, a British sherry promotion; he sees posters plastered across the great windows and electronic sliding doors; he perceives that these are all surface things, that there is no substance to such garish stimulation. They are not beautiful the way the rivers of heaven are beautiful; but why do none of the people around him appear to acknowledge this? Why do they not cry out that they have been robbed of what is true and living, left to make do with earthbound things and tawdriness and mere distractions? Unable to articulate his sorrow in any other way, he screams for liberation from it all. He does not yet realise that he is here to stay.

4.

Through one of her health visitors, Stella got a job at a private hospital in the West End. It was in CSSD, which – though she had difficulty in remembering it – stood for Central Sterile Supply Department. Her job was to pack instruments and swabs in big plastic bowls and put them in a machine called an autoclave which sterilised them. She also had to open the bags of laundry that came into the operating theatres twice a day, sort out the clean clothes and sheets and fold them up in a special way. She worked in a small, stark white room with a narrow table in the middle and cupboards full of the different things that needed to go into bowls. The air in the room was warm and dry.

Anna, the other woman in CSSD, was ten years older. She was large and bosomy and didn't say very much, partly because she was Italian and didn't speak English well, but mainly because she liked to keep herself to herself. Her favourite phrase – used with a sigh whenever another load of laundry came in or Sister had told them off for getting behind – was '*Molto travaglio, poco denario*', which one of the nurses translated as 'A lot of work, little money'. Stella learnt to say it too, and it became their team motto, binding them together.

Many of the people who worked in the hospital were foreign, to such an extent that Stella felt out of place in the changing room which she shared with theatre nurses. A lot of them came and went, because they were employed by an agency rather than the hospital, but they all seemed to be from the Philippines or India or Australia. Stella was in awe of them, and most of them ignored her to begin with; others were rude and said that English people didn't know what it was to work hard. A lot of the patients were foreign too, and Stella sometimes came across small groups of Arab women in dark headscarves sitting anxiously in corridors. She wondered if they were harems.

She couldn't get used to the idea of being a member of staff rather than a patient, though this hospital was different from the one in which she had given birth to Kit. The entrance was like a smart hotel's, and one of the porters told her that the cost of spending the night was several hundred pounds. The best thing was the canteen, which was very expensive for visitors but cheap for staff. There was always meat and fish to choose from and lots of vegetables and chips, heaped in stainless steel compartments as if in a giant till.

Apart from her lunch break, all her time from eight in the morning until five in the afternoon was spent in the basement. There were no windows in CSSD, and sometimes she would begin to feel claustrophobic and have to find an excuse to walk about a bit.

Next to CSSD were six operating theatres. On her way past she would glimpse the nurses – barely recognisable in their facemasks and surgical gowns – grouped around tables; but she could never have brought herself to look closely at what was going on, even if she hadn't been afraid of being reprimanded by Sister. Nor could she bear to think that people's lives were tugging at their moorings a few yards away as she went about her daily chores, or that the instruments she packed and sterilised would actually be used to probe their bodies. Once, when a nurse came into CSSD with a small circular saw which still had blood on it, Stella thought she was going to sick.

She found the job stressful and difficult. There were different packs to be prepared for different operations, and you had to remember what the instruments were called and make sure that there were the right number, and they all had to be put together in a certain way so that the nurses could find everything immediately. It was easy to forget a towel or little bundle of swabs. Luckily Anna knew it all by heart and kept an eye on her; but sometimes a nurse would come in needing something urgently when Anna was on her lunch break, and Stella would have to put it together by herself and spend the rest of the day terrified, thinking that she must have forgotten a vital instrument and that she was going to lose her job.

Once the contents of a pack had been assembled, it had to be wrapped in special green crêpe paper, put on a trolley and pushed into the autoclave. The machine had a big, thick metal door like the safes in films about bank robberies, and you had to turn a handle to close it and watch the dials to see that the pressure was right. That was worrying too, and Stella sometimes had nightmares about it blowing open in her face. When everything had been sterilised and you opened the door again, you had to be careful because the trays were hot and you could easily burn yourself on them.

The most boring thing was folding surgical gowns and big green rubberised sheets for use in the operating theatres. That had to be done in a special way as well, so even though they had been folded by someone else at the laundry you had to shake them out and start all over again. Sometimes there were bloodstains which hadn't quite come out and you had to send them back for another wash.

It was an exhausting job. You had to stand up all day, and your legs got tired and your back ached. Stella felt silly too in the disposable cap and short white gumboots she had to wear with her pink trousers and short-sleeved shirt. And she missed Kit.

Kit! Sometimes – too often – she stopped in the act of folding the green paper and wondered what she was doing there without her child. She began to imagine that he was dead and panicked and had to gasp for air. Separation was like a second pregnancy: just as she had carried him in her womb, always aware of him even if only subconsciously, so now she carried his absence. When she took him to the child-minder in the morning, she had to thrust him at the woman and turn away, making the procedure as automatic as possible in case determination failed her. At work she ached for his smile and the kicking motion of his small legs. From time to time, when she was alone for a few minutes, she would just let herself go, and cry and cry.

'Checkmate,' said Mr Czernowsky.

I looked at him in disbelief. I'd only lost a bishop and a handful of pawns; surely all I needed to do was take his knight... but no, it was just out of reach. Well then, I could move my king back...

I reached out and touched the wooden cross with my fingertips. It was no good: I was hemmed in by my own pieces. His rook was a safe distance in front of me. I was left with the forward diagonal squares, one covered by his knight, the other by a pawn. It *was* checkmate.

'I'm afraid you're right,' I said.

He gave a little chuckle. It was our third game of the day, and I was getting worse rather than better. The tips I'd got from Dick Mildmay over late-night games at his flat in South Kensington seemed to have stayed with me only as long as the next morning's hangovers.

Perhaps, I thought, I'd do better after lunch: an hour at The Goat, sticking to bitter lemon, would allow me to regroup my thoughts. But when I suggested an adjournment, Czernowsky insisted on transferring the game to his pocket board and taking it with us; no sooner had my steak-and-kidney pudding arrived than I had lost once more.

It had been a shock to set foot in the cottage again. Not that he'd done anything to it that would have seemed terrible to outsiders; they might even have preferred his durable rugs to my parents' threadbare carpets. But the sight of that familiar shell filled with unfamiliar shapes and colours made me feel as dizzy as if I'd stepped into one of those spinning fairground rooms where centrifugal (or is it centripetal?) force pins you to the wall while the floor recedes. I was bewildered, disorientated, miserable. Rows of blue and white plates were spread across the dresser like an army of occupation; curtains reeking of cigarette smoke lurked beside the windows; photographs in scuffed leather frames crowded the surface of a side-table.

I especially resented the photographs. But, I told myself, there was no point in getting angry: I was here to set the situation to rights. I was here to win.

To my surprise, Czernowsky was more than happy to talk during our games. He chatted freely about politics, gardening, sport, the Romantic poets – and proved remarkably well-informed. But he never returned to the subject of his own life. Eventually I asked him why.

'What is the point?' he replied. 'I am not a historian. When you get to my age you will realise that reminiscence is a dangerous thing. Too many old people turn in upon themselves: they shrink instead of growing. Perhaps I do not have as much to look forward to as I once did; but I am content to live for the day.'

'I have an awful feeling,' said Dick Mildmay when I reported this conversation, 'that you may be shooting yourself in the foot. The more games of chess he gets, the less likely he is to go gaga. You're giving him a reason to keep going – perhaps adding years to his life.'

I was afraid he might be right.

'You know what this reminds me of?' my opponent said one day. '*The Seventh Seal,* where the knight plays chess against Death.'

'I'm flattered. Next time I'll wear a cowl and white make-up.'

'You would make a good fell sergeant, I think.'

'Sorry?'

'The fell sergeant, Death. *Hamlet.*'

'Ah.'

'You need to lose a little weight, though. Anyway, we are not in the fells here, we are in the Cotswolds.'

He seemed to find this terribly funny. I consoled myself with the thought that Death always won in the end.

Kit is beginning to get used to separation from his mother; he no longer wails when she kisses him quickly and propels him towards the child-minder. Mrs Ragg is fascinating because she is black. She is a kind woman, and although her arms do not provide as frequent and as warm a cocoon as his mother's, they are well practised in holding babies. He feels safe in them.

Her house is full of bright, intriguing objects. But most intriguing of all are the other children she looks after – one a boy of about the same age as Kit, the other a slightly younger girl. The difference in sex means nothing to Kit, but he prefers the girl's company because she is even less familiar with this world than he is; the boy, on the other hand, seems interested in nothing but new shapes and new sounds.

'What do you remember?' Kit asks her silently as they lie side by side, searching each other's eyes. 'Do you remember the fields?'

'Yes,' she says, 'I remember the fields. I remember the thick grass, greener than anything here, wet and gleaming with dew, bathing my feet with coolness. I remember that green stretching far and wide, out towards fragrant hedgerows, and the flowers that sprang up across them – daffodils and poppies and daisies and fritillaries and primroses and a thousand stranger, rarer things that could not flourish here, caressed by bees and kissed by butterflies; and when I lay on the grass, the other creatures busy on its broad stalks: the slow beetles and dizzy ants and portly ladybirds. I remember how sweet and quaint their song was as they hurried about their tasks, singing in small, thin voices: crude compared to angels' voices, but tuned in their rough way to the music of the spheres. I loved to watch them, the smallest of God's creatures, all eager to fulfil their tiny roles.

'And I loved the cliffs of heaven – those great cliffs rising above the strand, white against blue, like pillars of the firmament. The gulls that gathered on their gleaming ledges wheeled joyfully through cool air, as if weightless, on their taut wings; strong-rooted trees blossomed in the fissures. And from the summit, how far you could gaze, out across shining tracts of ocean, knowing that nothing there was beyond one's reach, but nothing was circumscribed: that all one sought was found; that yearning and its fulfilment remained in dynamic tension, with the sweetness of anticipation forever undiminished by attainment. The sunbeam on the ridge of water, always yours to chase and grasp and chase once again – that is what I miss; because in this place I am aware of longings that cannot be satisfied, or those that are satisfied only to give place to new ones; and I recognise that the infinite is not known as our home; that it is seldom thought about, and often misunderstood, and even feared.' Her eyes fill with tears.

'Don't cry,' says Kit. 'We are still part of it. We will return.'

'I know that. But every day my awareness of it diminishes, and memory grows less distinct. Every day I am worn down by the demands of this body and seduced further from the reality of heaven. Don't you feel it? This is our dilemma: the better we learn to cope with this world, the further removed we become from our own, and that is what breaks my heart. If only we could communicate with these outcasts, repay them for their love by reminding them of where they came from and what they have lost! But they cannot learn our language; instead, we must mimic theirs, and follow their ways, and pour our energy into coping with the most basic functions.

'And when we find some link with heaven – some object of beauty that mirrors the beauty we have known – we cannot rejoice in it for long without remembering that the curse of transience is on it: that the tree will fall and rot, and the church decay, and our parents grow old and slow.'

Kit's eyes follow the movement of a branch which stretches across the window and throws its shadow against the wall.

'I suppose it is true,' he says. 'In this world, possibilities diminish; like you, I feel my life becoming more constrained with every advance I make. Whereas in heaven, the possibilities multiply, and to choose one path does not entail having to discard the rest.'

'But why, in the meantime, must we suffer in this truncated world?' she asks. 'Why have we been cast out? Why must we live a life before we return there?'

'I used to know,' says Kit. 'And it was the first thing I forgot.'

5.

Vicky David had the hard look of a woman who thought she was beautiful. In the normal course of events, I would not on principle have given her a second glance. But when she was presented to me as my future mother-in-law, there was nothing I could do except stare.

'Come to lunch on Saturday,' Dad had said on the phone. 'I've got something to tell you.' I immediately feared the worst; and when I walked into the drawing-room and saw champagne cooling in an ice bucket, my suspicions were confirmed. I looked instinctively towards Vicky's left hand: it was weighed down by an engagement ring as brash and shiny as the Lloyd's Building.

'Vicky and I have decided to get married,' Dad said. 'We wanted you to be the first to know.'

You don't fool me, I thought: you've asked me here because you feel you have to – and I'm probably the last person in London to be told. But I forced myself to smile and say, 'Congratulations.'

'Thank you, Sebastian.'

'Have you set a date for the wedding?'

'Not yet,' said Vicky. 'But we don't want to hang around.' The 'we' struck a chill to my heart. 'We're neither of us getting any younger,' she added archly.

'Speak for yourself, darling,' said my father, wrapping the bottle of champagne in a napkin. 'This girl's given me a whole new lease of life, Sebastian.'

He was certainly looking very spry, with his white Levi's, black polo-neck, sports jacket and slicked-back hair.

'You'd better not get too much younger,' said Vicky. She passed her hand lightly across his bottom as he handed me a glass. 'I want a mature older man, not a sex-mad toy boy.'

He chuckled smugly. 'Vicky's got me to join a fitness club. It's a wonderful place. I go there for an hour every day – do some running, a bit of weight-training. I haven't felt this good since I was at school. You should try it.'

I was tempted to point out that I didn't have thirty years of business lunches to work off. Instead I said that I got plenty of exercise carrying lights and tripods.

'I go along most days to keep an eye on him,' said Vicky. 'You never know what he might get up to with all those bimbos in leotards.'

I took a long gulp of champagne and wondered what it had been like when Dad got engaged to Mum. I think they were rather poor at the time, so perhaps they merely went out to a coffee bar to celebrate with Robbie; or maybe they splashed out on a bottle of wine and drank it on the deck of a pleasure boat going down the Thames, wrapped in sheepskin coats, with black-and-white scenery behind them.

'Where's the wedding going to be?'

'Chelsea Town Hall,' said my father. 'Maybe lunch at the Ritz afterwards. Just a small affair.'

'And are you going to carry on living here?'

This kind of conversation, as Robbie once explained to me, is known among linguists as 'phatic communication'. Neither party is really interested in what the other is saying – it's merely a ritual. There was no reason why Dad and Vicky should move out of this perfectly nice Kensington house, and even if they did, I couldn't have cared less. It wasn't as if I popped round there every night for a bite of supper and some fatherly advice.

'For the time being,' said Vicky. 'But it might be a bit cramped when you have some little brothers and sisters.'

I raised my eyebrows. I knew from Dick Mildmay that she was a ruthless office politician; yet here she was, acting a combination of sex kitten and saccharine little woman. Lady Macbeth could have passed herself off more successfully as Little Nell. But – well, she *was* fooling the only person that mattered, and that was my father. He was living a fantasy in which this Amazon who would submit to nobody else had fallen beneath his spell, and he was loving it.

At lunch she insisted on waiting on us hand and foot. 'Don't move, boys,' she said, 'I know you've got lots to talk about.'

Of course Dad and I didn't have lots to talk about. What I wanted to know from him was whether he had told Mum about his forthcoming marriage and how he had enjoyed his last encounter with Robbie; instead, I feigned an interest in the politics of his agency, and he tried to discuss my career without losing his temper.

'Done any interesting shoots lately?' he asked.

'I did a portrait of Andrea Meissen for *Frontier*.'

'Oh. How's it doing, that magazine?'

'Not too badly. I think they're selling around 60,000 copies a month. They used my picture on the cover, which was quite exciting.'

'I'll ask my secretary to dig it out for me. She's not much of an actress, is she, Andrea Meissen? One of those women who become famous over here for a couple of sitcoms, but could never begin to make it in the States.'

'I wish you'd been there to tell her that. What a prima donna.'

'What are you working on next? More snaps of debs?'

I told him about the mushroom project – which was just beginning to get under way – without letting on that my partner was Robbie's girl-friend.

'Mushrooms!' he exclaimed. 'Who's going to want to buy a book about mushrooms?'

'All sorts of people,' I said, affronted. 'People who go hunting for them, or like reading about food, or like brilliant photographs. Those kinds of books sell tens of thousands of copies. You should know that.'

'Only if they're written by celebrities.'

'Which we will both be when it becomes a bestseller. '

'It's more likely to end up in one of those short-lease shops with a poster saying "Book Bargains" across the window.'

'There's always that risk. At least we're making an effort. Would you rather I was just sticking these pictures into an album?'

'I'd rather you got some proper work. How much money do you think you're going to get from this? Four figures if you're lucky. You could be earning that much in a week if you got off your backside and played your cards right.'

I said nothing, which only made him angrier.

'That's right!' he exploded. 'Don't bother to answer! Just sit there feeling bloody superior, too stuck-up to dirty your hands with the same work as your father. Well, take a look at yourself – ten years into your profession and where are you going? Nowhere. It's a good job for Vicky that she's marrying me and not you, because you couldn't *begin* to support her. Wake up, Sebastian! Country Gold margarine fed you! Shazam washing powder clothed you! Lustre shampoo put you through school! So get down off your bloody high horse.'

'I'd rather have been fed by *Blow Up*,' I said.

'Oh you would, would you? Well excuse *me* for not being Antonioni! Jesus Christ!'

Vicky wandered blithely back into the room, like a botanist peering at poppies in no man's land.

'What's all this about?' she asked in a nannyish voice as she forced the plunger of the cafetière down.

'Sebastian was wishing Antonioni had been his father.'

'Tony who?'

'He's determined to end up like his uncle. I'm afraid we'll have to have a whip-round and buy him a houseboat.'

I took the opportunity to change the subject.

'I've been going down to the cottage quite a lot,' I said, and I told them about my chess matches with Czernowsky. 'You used to play a bit, didn't you, Dad?'

'Not really,' he said. 'Delicious coffee, darling. Well done on getting that new grinder.'

Dad, I thought, you've been watching too many commercials.

Stella's favourite person at the hospital was Clyde. He was a short West Indian with a perpetual smile, older than most of the staff; his job included acting as a go-between for CSSD and the nurses upstairs. Two or three times a day he would wheel his stores trolley into the room where Stella worked and sing out a list of what he had or what he wanted, like Lonnie Donegan performing *The Rock Island Line*:

'I got swabs, I got clamps, I got cardiac catheter packs...'

When he wasn't being Lonnie Donegan he would do his Harry Belafonte impression, inviting Stella or Anna to come and live with him on his island in the sun. Anna, who thought him a buffoon, would turn her back, shaking her head and mumbling in Italian, which only encouraged him to greater absurdities; but Stella thought him funny and charming, and liked the idea of him sitting on a silver beach mending his fishing nets and crooning to the sleepy tumble of waves on the lagoon. He never stayed for more than a few minutes, because Sister had told him off for spending too much time gossiping, and she had her eye on him; but occasionally Stella bumped into him in the canteen, and he told her mad stories about his family in Jamaica and the things they got up to when they had had too much rum, which seemed to be most of the time.

'My Uncle Barney,' he said, 'he was the worst of the lot. He loved his rum, and he loved betting – he'd take a bet that the sun wouldn't rise tomorrow if you gave him long enough odds. He was a great, great cricketer too. He could have been a professional, but the night before his trial for a big team in Kingston, a man bet him he couldn't drink a pint of rum over breakfast. By the time he got to the cricket ground you could have put a match to his mouth and burnt half the sugar cane in the Caribbean. He still played a fine game, mind you; but the club had him marked down as trouble, and that was that.'

Stella found this rather sad. 'Poor bloke,' she said.

'Well, yes and no,' said Clyde, suddenly serious. He had a quiet voice when he wasn't singing. 'Sure, drink can be an awful thing, and it can ruin lives and families. But I don't think Uncle Barney would necessarily have been a happier man if he had played for the West Indies. A richer one, maybe; but he still managed to support his wife and children, and he was never vicious or quarrelsome when he was drunk, and though some people shook their heads at his behaviour, everybody loved him – so who are we to say that he threw his life away? Judge not lest ye be judged.'

'My gran used to say that to me.'

'Then your gran was a very wise woman.'

'Oh she was, yeah. Always full of sayings. "Sufficient unto the day is the evil thereof" – that was one of her favourites. I never had no idea what it means though.'

'I believe it means that you shouldn't bear grudges. Start every day with a clean slate.'

'Oh,' said Stella. 'Funny way of putting it.'

'You're right,' replied Clyde with a chuckle. 'The Bible has very funny ways of putting things. Are you a church-goer?'

'Me. Oh no.' She answered as if he had asked her whether she spent her holidays on the Riviera. 'My gran and granddad was, though. They always made us go when we was with them.'

'My uncle – not the one who played cricket, mind – he was a minister. He used to preach a sermon like nobody, full of hellfire. People said it was better than going to horror films, except you couldn't buy ice-cream in the interval. I used to sit there shaking in my shoes. I was in the choir, of course, having such a fine singing voice.' He broke into a falsetto: *'The Lord's my shepherd, I'll not want…'*

'Ssh!' said Stella, looking round in embarrassment. 'Everyone will hear you. You're mad, you are.'

'So they tell me.' He started to sing again: *'Mad about the boy…'*

Stella couldn't help but laugh.

'So tell me, Stella,' he said, stacking baked beans on to a slice of sausage, 'how long have you been married?'

She looked down at the ring which she wore on her wedding finger for the sake of appearances. 'Two years,' she said. 'Only he's in the Army, see? So I don't get to see him very much.'

'Where's he posted, then?'

'Oh, he goes all over the place.' She searched her mind desperately. 'He's in Northern Ireland now.'

'You must be very worried about him.'

'Yeah. Yeah, I am.'

'And he must miss his little boy.'

'Yeah.' She felt awful lying to Clyde, getting all this sympathy under false pretences. But she wasn't going to have anyone in this hospital sneering at Kit because he was illegitimate; and though she didn't think Clyde would sneer, he might tell somebody else who would.

'Still, Kit is very lucky to have a proper father at all,' said Clyde. 'A lot of kids don't these days. What's your husband's name?'

'Ken.' Oh God, she wished it were true. Perhaps if she said it enough it *would* be true. Life would be so easy if only she had Ken. 'You married?'

It was not a question she had asked any of her colleagues before; somehow she found it impossible to imagine them having lives outside the hospital. She would have been shocked if Clyde had said yes, but instead he shook his head.

'No,' he said. 'That's why I come flirting with all you pretty ladies.' He winked at her. 'Better keep my distance with you, though, hadn't I? Else your soldier sweetheart will come and beat me up.'

I don't think I have ever been colder than I was that day in my uncle's studio. Robbie, dressed in an overcoat that reached his ankles, was skipping with remarkable agility from one end of an enormous canvas to another, adding dabs of paint with a brush that was almost invisible in his fingerless-mittened hand. The subject of the painting, as far as I could make out, was an albatross homing in on the Northern Lights. I wondered whether it had been inspired by the Arctic conditions in which he worked.

'It's called *Tripping the Light Fantastic*,' said Sabrina. 'Brilliant, isn't it?'

She grinned at me, her eyes sparkling behind National Health glasses. The contrast with my future stepmother could not have been stronger. Sabrina was so careless of her beauty that it would never have occurred to her to wear contact lenses. Her hair was thin and golden, her skin flawless.

It was actually her that I'd come to see, to discuss our mushroom book. When Robbie had put his brushes away and we were thawing out in the pub on the corner, I unzipped my portfolio and produced my first study of a photogenic fungus. The specimen was an unremarkable puffball, but after weeks of experimenting with different cameras, lenses, films, papers and developing techniques, I had come near to achieving the effect I was looking for – a photograph which presented the mushroom not as a cloned supermarket item on a chopping board but something with a life of its own, something primeval and unpredictable rearing out of nothingness. The black-and-white film had a luminosity suggesting, I hoped, a secretive nocturnal activity of which the camera was a privileged voyeur. There was also, as Sabrina was quick to remark, a hallucinogenic quality about it.

'Wow,' she said. 'It's like you're giving back to the mushroom the magic that's inside it. It's like you've photographed its aura.'

'It's something else,' said Robbie. 'It's art with a capital "A". This is the most important thing you've done in your entire life.'

He couldn't have paid me a higher compliment, and I grinned as its warmth stole through me.

'I think it's becoming an obsession with a capital "O",' I said. 'I'd like to make a video capturing the whole cycle of growth and decay. But no one would watch it. Anyway, it's more challenging to try and pin down the key moment – the instant of change, if it exists.'

'I bet that's how Andy Warhol got started,' said Sabrina. 'I bet he tried to do exactly the same thing but couldn't, and in frustration decided to turn all the mushrooms into soup, and then had the idea of painting soup cans.'

'I'll buy that,' I said. 'What do you think, Robbie?'

'Warhol? Oh, Warhol did his own thing.' He suddenly seemed restless. 'Let's go to the Arts Club. Got your wheels, Silver Surfer?'

When I first visited the Chelsea Arts Club, it was my idea of heaven. You rang the bell beside an inconspicuous door in an ordinary London street and were admitted to a world over which the changing values of the city outside appeared to have no dominion. This was Bohemia – a small, precious enclave where Art reigned supreme and Convention pressed its nose to the window, and the great painters and writers of the day caroused and loved and debated passionately while the ghost of Dylan Thomas helped itself to another drink behind the bar. Here I came in awe, and soon began to fidget.

Perhaps it was because I began to suspect that I was far more conventional than I thought. I loved the *idea* of sitting up all night with an internationally acclaimed sculptor, a concrete poet who'd lived with Allen Ginsberg and a mysterious girl in a leather mini-skirt who chain-smoked Gauloises, listening to tales of Greenwich Village and the Rive Gauche; but somehow when it came down to it the sculptor always seemed to be a bore, and the poet had wandering-hand trouble, and the girl kept cadging money for her next packet of twenty. It was the difference between a bottle of champagne and a hangover, akin to the realisation that *The Rubaiyat of Omar Khayyam* is not a great romantic credo but the maudlin ramblings of an Arab wino. I began to look on the Arts Club as a home for lost souls, more limbo than paradise. But that isn't to say that I didn't continue to be fascinated by it; and when I went there, I was reminded that for every lost soul who dissipated his talent in drink, there was someone else with a tougher constitution who thrived in this shadowland and might never have succeeded without its raffish inspiration.

The place was quiet this particular evening apart from a boisterous pair of illustrators at one of the pool tables in the bar, and the girl in charge of the dining-room had no difficulty in seating us. Sabrina and I ordered mushroom risotto in honour of our project; Robbie chose chicken Marengo.

'Delicious,' he said when it arrived. 'The bird has met its Waterloo. So tell me, when's the wedding?'

'At the end of next month,' I said. 'Are you going?'

'I'll decide on that when I know if I'm invited. How about you – going to take the official photographs?'

'No thanks. They can hire one of those little old men with a plate camera who keeps the couple signing the register for ten minutes. I'll have enough to worry about.'

'I can't imagine one of my parents getting married again,' said Sabrina. 'And I certainly can't imagine being there.'

'I'm afraid I stopped being interested in my father's girlfriends a long time ago. To begin with I saw them all as potential stepmothers; then I realised that Dad wasn't going to rush into marriage again, and I stopped worrying. But I must say, now that it's happening, I can't help wishing he'd chosen someone else.'

'I think I'll have to go, just out of curiosity,' said Robbie. 'If they don't invite me I'll turn up at the town hall and throw rice at them any-way – egg-fried rice.'

'Robbie!'

A tall man in a tweed suit had just entered the room. His arm was raised in an extravagant gesture, so that he half resembled a dictator saluting his cohorts and half an actor inviting applause.

'Desmond!'

The stranger gave a small bow and advanced towards us. He had a thin, angular body, which – combined with a sharp nose and thick, brushed-back grey hair – gave the impression of a stork blessed with a top-class tailor. He had probably been good-looking as a young man, but his eyes had now retreated behind a barricade of wrinkles.

'Desmond, this is Sabrina,' said Robbie. 'Sabrina, Desmond Hilton.'

Hilton gave another bow, took Sabrina's hand, and kissed it. 'Sabrina fair,' he murmured. 'How do you do?'

I shuddered. There was something almost murderous about that kiss: it reminded me of a print of Death and the Maiden. If ever there was a reason for not coming to the Arts Club, this man was surely it.

'And this is Sebastian, my nephew.'

Hilton raised an eyebrow as he gave me a handshake like wet cardboard. 'Ah,' he said, 'Tony's boy.'

'That's right.'

'May I join you?'

'Course you can,' said Robbie. 'Grab a chair. Belinda,' he called to the waitress, 'can we have another glass?'

'Have you been having supper here?' Sabrina asked.

'Sadly not. Neither my stomach nor my wallet can accommodate the overpriced delicacies served up by the beautiful Belinda. But she lets me pass from table to table begging crusts at the end of the evening.'

'Porkies,' said Robbie. 'You'll find him here every night, happily tucking away three courses with a double portion of mashed potato, and he never puts on an ounce of weight, unlike the rest of us. He's Belinda's best customer.'

Despite this, Belinda didn't seem particularly thrilled with him. She slammed down the glass, fended off a hand that was moving to pat her on the bottom and stomped away towards the kitchen. When the glass had been filled, Hilton took a gulp and then settled it on his knees, staring at it as if he expected it to turn into water the moment he took his eye off it.

It's always amazing to me that someone as nice and intelligent as my uncle should have time for people as obviously worthless as Desmond Hilton. Perhaps it's pity – perhaps Hilton was a once brilliant and successful man whose life had been undermined by unknown tragedies; and perhaps Robbie, as a former junkie, had an understanding of his type which only that kind of experience can bring. But the truth is that some people are so forgiving of others' shortcomings that they are almost completely undiscriminating in their friends.

'God, I've had a day of it,' said Hilton.

'What happened?' asked Sabrina.

'Oh, all very boring for you, gracious lady. I've been looking after a house for some friends, and someone was supposed to be coming this morning to take the piano off and restore it, and at ten to one he rang to say there'd been some accident with the van and he wouldn't be able to come until tea time. So then I had to sit there until four o'clock waiting for him. As it happened, I didn't have anything urgent to do – '

Robbie laughed. 'The day Desmond has something urgent to do,' he said, 'they'll turn this place into a business centre.'

' – but it could have been damned inconvenient. Then when he did turn up he asked me to give them a hand shifting the bloody thing. Really unprofessional. I mean, it doesn't make any difference to me, but I hate to think of Caroline and Tom relying on someone like that. I bet he's ripping them off something rotten. Then I went to Christie's South Ken and there wasn't a thing worth looking at.'

'Sounds like a hell of a day,' I said.

'Do you deal in furniture?' asked Sabrina.

'I deal in everything, dear lady – in furniture, paintings, erotica, hopes and dreams…'

'You used to deal in some good grass too,' said Robbie.

'Not an occupation for a gentleman any more. Do you see me with a Rottweiler at my heels and a baseball bat under my pillow?'

'I think they'd rather suit you,' said Sabrina.

He took her hand and kissed it again. 'Isn't she sweet?'

'Anyone at the bar?' asked Robbie.

'Peter Edelman hoping that someone will buy him a drink; Angela Wilton with her toy boy. It's not exactly the Bloomsbury Group – more a *salon des refusés*. What's the news from the artistic front line?'

Robbie gave him a run-down of his work in progress. Sabrina and I discussed our book. Eventually the waitress came back. 'Any more drinks from the bar?' she asked.

'I think we're all right,' I said.

'I might just manage a brandy, darling,' said Hilton. She glared at him and marched off.

'I've got an early start tomorrow,' I lied. 'Shall we get the bill when she comes back?'

Hilton looked at me as if noticing me for the first time. 'So you're Tony's boy?'

'That's right.'

'I hear he's getting married again. Who's the lucky girl?'

'She's called Vicky David. Works in the City. Mid-thirties.'

'Pretty?'

'OK.'

'Of course she is. I know Tony. They're always pretty.'

The arrival of his brandy shut him up temporarily. I couldn't help comparing him with Dick Mildmay: though they were roués of the same vintage, the excesses that one managed to make attractive, the other made repellent. They were as different as sun and shadow.

The bill came. 'Anyone going south?' asked Hilton.

'Sebastian's going to Battersea,' said Robbie. 'He can take you.'

'Sure,' I said reluctantly. 'Where do you live?'

'This place I'm looking after is in Wandsworth. Shouldn't be too far out of your way. It's a nice little house, but it's cost me a bloody fortune in taxi fares.'

The nice little house was, of course, enormous, and about as far away from my flat as you could get without leaving the borough.

'I've never been a south-of-the-river man myself,' said Hilton as we headed into uncharted territory.

'It's all right.'

'Nice bundle of goods, young Sabrina. Robbie's done well for himself.'

I didn't answer, but wished I'd turned the tape deck on loud when we got into the car.

'He wasn't a bad painter in his day,' he continued.

'I don't think he's got any worse. In fact I'd say his work's improved. Unfortunately for him, tastes have changed.'

'You're very friendly with him, aren't you?'

'Yes,' I said, 'I am.'

'I'm surprised.'

I glanced at him. 'Why?'

'Well, after what happened between him and your father, I wouldn't have thought Robbie would want anything to do with your part of the

46

family.'

I said nothing for a moment. Whatever was coming, I wasn't sure that I wanted to hear it. But in the end I took a deep breath and asked, 'What exactly *did* happen between him and my father?'

'You mean you don't know?'

'No.'

To my surprise, he backed off. 'Well, no one's absolutely sure, but the word is that your father treated your uncle pretty badly.'

So he had simply been angling, hoping that I would open the family secrets to him. I was tempted to stop the car then and there, and make him walk the rest of the way. Instead, I turned on the tape deck.

The next day I rang Robbie and told him about our conversation.

'Don't take any notice of Desmond,' he said. 'He just likes stirring – or trying to.' But for my uncle he sounded pretty unrelaxed.

Clyde invited Stella to spend Sunday with him at Kew Gardens. It would be good for Kit to have an outing, he said: surely her husband wouldn't object to that?

Stella liked the idea. She couldn't remember whether she'd ever been to Kew – she vaguely thought that her grandfather might have taken her there as a girl – but it *sounded* so green and leafy, and so different from the hopeless patches of grass near the estate where she usually took Kit at weekends. It would certainly do him good; and though she wasn't sure what she felt about spending time with Clyde, it didn't have to mean anything while she was under the protection of her make-believe husband. So she said yes.

On her own, she would have dismissed such an expedition out of hand, because of the difficulties of taking Kit on the bus with all the bottles and nappies and wipes that he needed. But Clyde had a car and said he would pick her up, even though it meant a detour halfway across London from where he lived in Ealing. He told her that he would come at twelve o'clock, after church.

She didn't want him to see her dilapidated flat, so she was downstairs with the buggy at a quarter to. He arrived in an old Vauxhall Viva, and she nearly burst out laughing when she saw him in his weekend clothes: grey flannel trousers, a maroon V-neck and a white shirt. Not that he didn't look nice in them – he did; but any outfit would have seemed strange to her after the white coat he wore at work.

'So this is Kit,' he said, squatting down beside the buggy with a big smile. He held out a finger, which Kit grabbed eagerly. 'How do you do, young man? My name's Mr Foster, and most people call me sir, 'cept those silly nurses at the hospital who don't know a man of natural authority when they see one. But you can call me Clyde if you like, and if you don't mind, I'll call you Kit. This is a fine buggy you've got here, Kit. I bet you cut quite a dash in this neighbourhood, cruising around with wheels like these.'

Kit giggled.

'It's new,' said Stella. 'At least, it's new second-hand. There was this ad in the window of the newsagent's, see. It was a real bargain. I had an old pram before, and it was murder trying to get that in and out everywhere. It makes all the difference, this does.'

'Money well spent,' said Clyde. 'We had the parable of the talents in church this morning. I always enjoy that lesson. Now, Mr Kit, can we persuade you to leave that smart buggy and climb aboard this old jalopy of mine?'

They followed the thin Sunday traffic westwards. It was a light grey morning, with the sun almost pushing aside the clouds but then stopping short.

They parked at last beside the river, and Clyde paid for them to go into the gardens. He bought them lunch at the cafeteria too. Stella was dismayed at how expensive it was and kept saying that she wasn't hungry, but he insisted that it was his treat and that she was to have whatever she wanted.

She didn't know much about flowers. Her granddad had loved roses and had tried to teach her about the different kinds, but he had never had a garden to grow them in. He would have liked a job in a park, but had been too badly wounded in the War to do anything but the lightest of work. So he had sat in his chair evening after evening, looking through catalogues the nurseries sent him, putting crosses against the blooms he liked best as if he were actually going to buy them. Stella felt like crying when she thought of it.

In any case, it was not the flowers that made the greatest impression on her: it was the wide expanses of grass and trees with so much sky around them that it seemed they were anchored in blue and not green – that their branches were roots growing deeper into the ether and their roots branches supporting the ground. Or, if you accepted the force of gravity, they were sinewy old aboriginal men doing handstands. It was as good as being in the country, except for the aeroplanes that kept flying low over them. There were even squirrels and, to Kit's delight, ducks.

48

It started to drizzle, so they took shelter in a modern building called the Princess of Wales Conservatory. It was full of cactuses and other desert plants, rising from pebble-covered soil in dusty green colours and predominantly phallic shapes that made Stella feel embarrassed. Nor did she like the wicked thorns and deceptive down that covered them, feeling sure that at any moment a child would stumble into one of them and have to be carried away shrieking and bleeding. She was glad that Kit was strapped into his buggy.

After that they went to the great glass and wrought-iron Palm House. Clyde said that it had been built in Victorian times, and Stella thought how strange it must have seemed to the first visitors, coming face to face with gigantic plants they had only read about. Even to her, who had seen them on television, it was an extraordinary place, with the light pulled away into an origami of leaves and the air so humid that you felt you could take a handful and wring it out on to the tiles. Kit seemed to find it particularly uncomfortable and to Stella's alarm started to go red in the face, so they took him down to the aquarium, where Clyde had heard that there were alligators.

As it turned out, there was nothing approaching the size of an alligator; but the tanks of small, strange fish which they found instead were so hypnotising that reptiles were forgotten in a moment. Holding Kit up to the glass, Stella gazed as if she had never seen such colours before. There were fish of a luminous, purply blue that resembled floating fragments of pottery; goldfish like crystal vials encasing molten ore; a fish with a leopard-skin skirt of a tail which it flaunted as it minced across its tank. There were others so colourless as to be almost transparent, trailing long, delicate tendrils, or so flat as to be almost two-dimensional. One fixed them with an eye that swivelled backwards and forwards like a hinge on a pair of spectacles.

The fins, too, delighted her: in action they were a revelation, barely recognisable as the useless appendages which she had seen so often at the fishmonger's. Here they were busy little propellers, whirring through water; they extended like arms, semaphoring their owners' intentions. And what a contrast there was between the small fish, some with tails longer than their bodies, hunting through liquid space, and the larger ones, hanging virtually motionless, like floating tubers.

Looking behind her for a moment, she could see that everyone else, young and old, was as mesmerised as she was. Clyde caught her eye and grinned. 'You think this is something. You should see the sea around Jamaica – there are shoals of these things, pouring through the water like money out of a one-armed bandit.'

'They're all so... different,' Stella said.

He nodded. 'You have a simple thing like a fish, and you wouldn't think there was much point in fooling around with the basic design, and yet there are thousands of variations in size and form and colour. Well, that's God's creation for you: He could have just made those things so that they worked, but no, He decided to give us the strange and the beautiful too. They're here for our delight – hey Kit?'

Kit gurgled.

Outside, they stood for a moment on the edge of the ornamental lake. A handful of black swans came to look at them, and it seemed to Stella that, with their long, smooth necks and red beaks, they too might have passed for exotic plants.

It had been a good day, she thought as they loaded up Clyde's car. (Kit was fast asleep, and Clyde passed him carefully in to her.) What the consequences of it would be she wasn't sure, but if Clyde asked her out again she thought she would say yes.

As they drove back towards the flat, though, her spirits fell. The streets became tighter; the buildings seemed to close in around her. She had managed to forget the dreariness of her life for half a day, but now it was about to start again – the high-rise, graffiti, damp, and tomorrow work and separation from her child again. Perhaps those fish didn't have that great a time of it after all, imprisoned in their tanks, looking perpetually for the next scrap of food. *They* couldn't see how beautiful they were.

'Thanks ever so much,' she said when they arrived. 'I can manage from here.'

'Sure?'

'Yes. Thanks for everything.'

'That's my pleasure. See you tomorrow, then.'

'See you tomorrow.'

He waited until she was safely in the lift. She wished he hadn't, because it meant he could see her struggling and he would know that she really could have done with his help. But the thought was kind.

Upstairs, she tried to turn the key in the bottom lock, only to find it disengaged. That was odd: she could have sworn she'd followed the whole routine when she went out. She must have forgotten the last part of it in her anxiety to get down before Clyde arrived.

She turned the other key, and the door opened. Someone had turned the television on, and a six-pack of lager stood on the table.

6.

'Kenny! Oh, Ken!' There he was in front of the television watching snooker, of course. He looked harder than he had done when he went away, more muscular; but then, what else would you expect from the Army? His hair was different too: the duck-tail gone, replaced by a crew cut so severe that if she had seen him in a crowd she might not have registered that it was him. But he was still her Ken, and he was back. That was all that mattered.

In her dreams he had always got up at this point, taken her in his arms and whispered, 'I'm sorry, love, I'm sorry.' But he just sat there, gave her his little grin and said, 'Orright?' And yes, it was all right. She ran across and threw herself on his lap, flinging her arms around his neck, kissing his mouth, cheeks, neck, forehead.

'Careful!' he said, laughing as he felt for a safe place to put his can down. He gave her a long, deep kiss, then manoeuvred her round so that he could see the screen again.

She hadn't been able to bear watching snooker in his absence. Now she loved it again because he loved it – the smart clack of the balls, the players' deadpan faces as they chalked cues, the flourish with which the score was called.

'Who's winning?' she asked.

'Stevie,' he said. 'Bloody magic.'

She nestled against him, noticing a tattoo on his arm that hadn't been there before, blue lines framing a hand with a stubby sword.

'Good, innit?' he said. 'Bloke in Aldershot done it for me.'

'That where you been living?'

'Some of the time. Been moving around. I'm in the Army now.'

'I know.'

He looked at her suspiciously. 'How'd you know that?' he asked. 'You had spies after me or something?'

'Course not. Someone told me: Angie, that girl what works down the Albion. Her fiancé's in the Army. He seen you one time.'

'Yeah, well, I don't like being spied on. Stevie!'

Steve Davies was in control now; it seemed that no shot, however complex, could elude him. His opponent stood helplessly stroking his chin while the champion rattled his way to victory. 'Bloody magic,' said Ken.

This was the moment. 'Ken,' said Stella, 'come see the baby.'

'In a minute,' he said, not really registering the suggestion. His mouth clamped on hers; his hands tore at her clothes, stripping her to the waist. She too forgot Kit, letting Ken engulf her as he carried her into the next room and threw her down on to the bed.

When at last they lay still, she found herself wondering whether he would tell his Army friends about this. She knew that it was the kind of thing they talked about – but perhaps it was only pick-ups that really interested them, trophies of lust rather than love. She wondered too whether he had been unfaithful to her, then tried to drive the thought from her mind, knowing within herself that if she forced the question the answer would have to be yes. He wouldn't see it like that, though: he wouldn't admit that they had any relationship to be faithful to. Despair rushed through her like an underground train through its tunnel, over-whelming, deafening, dazzling. He hadn't come back to stay: if he had done, he surely would have expressed some regret, murmured some apology, not just thundered his way into her bed.

But no, she wasn't going to give in to such thoughts. She had him back, and now she was going to keep him. They were a family, the two of them and Kit. She could hear Kit waking up next door, giving some exploratory squeaks. When Ken saw his child, he must love him as she did herself.

'I'll just be a mo,' she said, finding her dressing gown and picking her way among the discarded clothes on the floor. In the sitting-room Kit sat up and waved his arms, agitating for liberation from his buggy. She gathered him up and carried him back to the bed.

'Look,' she said to Ken. 'Look at your little boy.'

'F--- me,' said Ken, gazing in amazement at Kit, who smiled and laughed. 'Cheerful little sod, ain't he?'

'You hold him.'

Ken took the baby gingerly, staring at his big eyes. 'Heavy, too. What you been feeding him? Pie and mash?'

Kit sneezed. Stella laughed, and reached out to wipe his nose. 'He likes you,' she said.

'Yeah, well he's got a funny bleeding way of showing it. Sneeze at you a lot, does he?'

He lifted Kit high in the air, and watched him kicking his legs. 'I tell you what,' he said, 'carry on like this and he'll be playing for Spurs in a few years. New bloody Lineker we've got here.'

Kit and Stella both laughed with delight. This was as it should be. They were all together at last.

'It's time for his bath,' said Stella. 'Ain't it, little love? Your dad don't know what he's in for. Wait till he sees you splashing around all over the place. You be a good boy now while I run it for you.'

Light with happiness, she went through into the bathroom. The flat was no longer a trap, but a staging-post on the way to better things. The worn carpet and the damp patch could be laughed at now. She thought of the Beatles' line 'It's getting better all the time', and hummed it as the water fell from the coughing taps. Then she went back to smile at the other two. Ken was pretending to arm-wrestle, his finger against Kit's fist.

'Where you been today then?' he asked.

'Kew Gardens,' said Stella. 'Magic, it was – all them trees and flowers. You liked it, didn't you, Kitty?'

'Go on your own, did you?'

'No, a mate from the hospital give us a lift. I'm working at a hospital now, see, up the West End. This bloke Clyde, he's really kind – said he'd take us for a day out.'

'Clyde! What kind of a bleeding name is that? He wouldn't last long in the regiment with a name like Clyde.'

'He's West Indian,' said Stella. 'They give them names like that.'

'Oh,' said Ken. His voice had become menacing, sarcastic. 'Nignog is he? You telling me that while I been off serving my country, you been taking my son off and going with a f---ing nignog?'

'He's a friend,' said Stella, angry and frightened now. 'Just a friend from the hospital.'

'Since when you been friends with nignogs, then? Good in bed, is he? Give you a good seeing to, does he? Well, I wonder whose f---ing kid this is.'

And to her horror he flung Kit down. The baby hit the edge of the bed and tumbled to the floor.

Kit screamed. Stella screamed, diving down beside him, taking him in her arms, sobbing, feeling for broken limbs. There didn't seem to be any, thank God, thank God. Ken turned away, pulling on his clothes.

'You could have killed him!' she shouted, her voice hysterical.

'Shut your face, you little tart,' he said, lacing his boots, 'or I'll kill you. I knew I didn't ought to have come.' He got to his feet, glaring down at her with such hatred that she felt sick.

'No, Kenny,' she said, getting up, still holding Kit to her. 'Don't go. Please don't go.'

He said nothing, drew back his hand, and slapped her across the cheek with such force that she fell on to the bed. As she lay there gasping, cradling her child, she heard the front door slam. Then there was nothing but the sound of running water, splashing hopelessly into the depths of the bath.

After Ken had gone, Stella went through the motions of washing Kit; or at least, she thought she must have done, because she found herself kneeling on the kitchen floor wrapping him in a towel, even though she couldn't remember testing the temperature of the water or placing him in the tub or handing him the red plastic boat which was his bath-time toy. When he was dry she put him into his sleep suit, but then instead of tucking him into his cot she sat with him on the couch, rocking him backwards and forwards, staring into space. The television was still on, and only when the national anthem was played to signal the end of the evening's programmes did she notice what time it was. As she slid into the disordered bed, she vaguely registered that her cheeks were grimy with dried tears.

She was still exhausted when she woke up. She moved through the morning routine on automatic pilot, giving Kit his breakfast, dressing him, dressing herself. But the memory of yesterday struck her with an almost physical force, and she sank to her knees, crying, choking, trying in vain to vomit. Ken would never come back now: that was the truth she must live with, that grotesque absence – and she just didn't want to, she wasn't going to; she would deny it and deny it, and somehow she would will things into rightness.

They were childish thoughts. Only when she pulled herself together did she really notice her own child's behaviour. Kit had not uttered a sound all morning: not a gurgle, not a laugh, not a cry. He had eaten the food put in front of him; he had submitted without protest to being dressed; now he was sitting on the floor doing nothing, staring at nothing as she had stared the night before.

'Kit!'

He didn't look at her when she called his name.

'Kit, love!' She picked him up, but there was still no response: no

54

clinging to her, no struggle for freedom. He sat motionless in her arms, staring at a vista that was closed to her.

Stella felt a gust of panic. She had been too quick to assume that Ken's brutal treatment of the child had done him no harm. The phrases 'brain damage' and 'internal bleeding' leapt violently into her mind like figures rung up on an old-fashioned cash register. She must take Kit to a doctor.

But how could she? How could she explain what had happened? She wasn't going to tell them that Ken was a child-batterer: it hadn't been like one of those terrible stories that you heard on the news. And even if she did, how could she be sure that they wouldn't hold her equally responsible – that they wouldn't take Kit away from her? She could say that it had been an accident, that he had fallen; but that was what child-batterers always said.

She needed time to think. She didn't have any, because she should have set off ten minutes ago on her journey to work via the child-minder's. But it was out of the question to leave Kit in his present state, and she steeled herself to ring the hospital and say that her baby was sick and she couldn't come in today. When she got through she asked to speak to Sister Murray, but Sister wasn't there and she had to leave a message. Then she rang the child-minder and told her that she had taken the day off and wouldn't be bringing Kit over.

The doctor's surgery closed at eleven. Stella passed the intervening hours in an agony of vacillation. At one moment she allowed herself to believe that nothing could be wrong with such a healthy-looking boy and that the doctor would be angry with her for wasting his time; at the next she imagined Kit lying unconscious on a hospital bed. Finally, at twenty to eleven, she bundled Kit into the buggy and hurried down the road to the health centre, only to be told that there were too many other people ahead of her in the queue. Was it an emergency? No, she said, it wasn't an emergency.

Clyde rang at lunchtime, his voice full of concern, to ask what was wrong with Kit and whether it had anything to do with their visit to Kew: had he caught a chill from being out in the air too long? Stella longed to tell him what had happened but was afraid that the reason for her argument with Ken would come out. She knew she couldn't bear that, not only because she didn't want Clyde to feel responsible, but because such an admission would signal a transfer of allegiance away from Ken; so she said that Kit had just got a bit of a temperature and the doctor had said it was nothing to worry about.

Nothing to worry about! In all her care-laden life, Stella had never felt as worried as she did on that long day. The anxiety was cumulative, for thinking about Kit and Ken made even the smallest domestic chores seem impossibly demanding. As she neglected them, they gathered together to lay siege to her conscience. When night came again, with no change in Kit, she felt drained and ill.

The next morning she did take him to the doctor. She said that she had gone to the park with a friend and one of the friend's children had accidentally released the brake of Kit's buggy and it had rolled down a slope and turned over with him inside. The doctor examined him and said that he'd probably just had a bit of a fright, but that if he wasn't behaving normally in a day or two he would send him to the hospital for some tests just to be on the safe side. Stella, though still anxious, felt better for having bitten the bullet and hugely relieved that the doctor had believed her story.

She was two hours late for work, and though she had telephoned the hospital to warn them, she thought she had better go to the sister's office on arrival to explain. To her dismay, Sister Murray was off today as well, and it was her less sympathetic deputy that she had to face.

'You knew Anna was taking a day's holiday yesterday, didn't you?' the woman said. With her hair drawn up under her cap, her stern expression was terrifying.

Stella had forgotten about Anna's holiday but didn't see that it made any difference. Kit had been ill and she'd had to look after him.

'Your absence was extremely inconvenient,' the woman continued. 'We ran out of cardiac catheter packs and had to get one of the theatre nurses to make them up. I had a look through the cupboards too, and the supply of bandages was deplorably low. You're going to have to pull your socks up.'

Kerry, one of the Australian nurses, advised Stella not to take too much notice: 'She's just a twisted old spinster. Women with babies make her feel inadequate.' But that afternoon Stella was summoned to see the personnel manager, who told her that she was being dismissed.

'Sister Tanner's opinion is that you are allowing your family responsibilities to interfere with your work and your department is failing to achieve its targets as a result. We're happy to employ working mothers here, but we can't make special allowances for them. You're on a week's notice, but we've decided to let you go on Friday.'

'But my baby was ill,' Stella protested. 'You can ask the doctor. It's not fair.'

'It's not my business to be fair. My business is to make sure that this hospital runs efficiently, and the simple fact is that you're not pulling your weight.'

Stella told Clyde over lunch in the canteen.

'Bitches!' he exclaimed. She had never seen him angry before. 'They've got someone else lined up for the job, that's what it is. One of the directors has a niece that wants to earn some holiday money, I bet; otherwise they wouldn't be in such a hurry to get rid of you.'

'If only Sister Murray was here,' said Stella. 'She'd stick up for me. She's always fair.'

Clyde shook his head. 'Too late for that now. She couldn't do anything without undermining Sister Tanner's authority. That's what these places are like.'

It was a custom in the theatres that anyone who was leaving bought a couple of bottles of wine to drink with the others. Stella didn't understand why it should be that way round – after all, she was the one who was going to have to watch every penny she had; but she went along with it, and at five o'clock on Friday afternoon the plastic cups were handed round from a concertina pile and those of the nurses and porters who weren't too busy came and stood around for a few minutes, sipping lukewarm Soave and feeling embarrassed. Anna showed a surprising degree of emotion, crying and giving Stella a big hug and murmuring blessings in Italian. By 5.30 the party was over; Stella changed and emptied her locker and then climbed the stairs to the street for the last time. It was an awful end to an awful week. She couldn't believe that only last Sunday she'd been watching those beautiful fish so happily in Kew Gardens.

Clyde was waiting for her on the pavement. 'I've got a leaving present for you,' he said, handing her a small gift-wrapped package. It was a cassette of gospel music. 'I think you'll enjoy it.'

'Ta,' she said, touched. 'Ta very much.'

'I'm not going to disappear, you know, just because we're not colleagues any more. I'll ring you up next week, if that's OK.'

'OK.'

'Bye then.' He kissed her on a cheek, and strode away with a wave.

'It is sometimes said,' remarked Mr Czernowsky, 'that hell is other people. There may be a certain amount of truth in that. But to my mind, hell is oneself.'

'What do you mean?'

'You are aware that I make a point of not living in the past, or rather trying not to. But there are times when I feel, like King Canute at the seaside, that my efforts are in vain and I am about to be overwhelmed by memories.'

'Any particular memories?' At last, I thought, he's actually going to divulge something: a wartime atrocity perhaps, or a murdered wife. But I was disappointed.

'The curious thing,' he said, 'is that when you reach my age there are some phases of your life that you can remember with extraordinary clarity, but others – often more recent – which have become totally obscured. In general, it is not the painful memories that fade, but the happy ones. When were you last ecstatically happy?'

'Um –'

'Exactly. As it happens, I would be able to answer that precisely: the 17th of June two years ago, when I beat Arthur Brecon after being reduced to my king, a knight and two pawns. But while I can remember the fact of that happiness, I cannot remember the happiness itself; whereas with things that one would prefer to forget, the memory can often be as intensely painful as the actual event. Check.'

I faced losing either a knight or a bishop. Which was it to be?

'I'm sorry you've had such a miserable time,' I said. 'But I'm glad you find some consolation in beating me.'

'I did not say that my life had been miserable: I think I have probably had a more enjoyable time than most people. My point is that when I stir the waters of memory, it is the disagreeable things that rise to the top – and they are things for which I myself must bear responsibility: small acts of selfishness, or opportunities that I failed to pursue.'

'Perhaps you're dead,' I said, 'and this is purgatory. You're atoning for your past mistakes by reliving them. After that, you can move on to heaven and spend eternity playing chess with the greats.'

He chuckled. 'That is a good idea. Certainly I do not derive the pleasure that you suppose from beating you. If the afterlife offers me worthier opponents, then I welcome it.'

I ignored the jibe and decided to part with my bishop. To my surprise and annoyance, he took a rook instead.

'And what about you?' he continued. 'What is your hell?'

'I think the traditional picture would do very well. However psychological we've become, physical pain takes a lot of beating. I'd be a hopeless spy – one prod with a lighted cigarette and I'd tell them anything they wanted to know.'

He took his spectacles off and polished them; then he put them on again and stared at me as if he was deciding whether or not to give me a job. 'I think that you are wrong,' he said. 'You seem to me a young man who decides what he wants and pursues it in a whole-hearted, if not totally effectual, way. I think that if you were committed to a cause, you would suffer for it with great courage – though personally I would never employ you as a spy, because you would be almost certain to get caught.'

However back-handed, it was the only compliment he ever paid me, and I was grateful for it. I don't agree about bad memories always rising to the top, because it is at that moment – rather than in one of his uncompromisingly prickly moods – that I tend to remember him.

I have to admit that I was beginning to find our perpetual challenge tedious. While I had become more interested in chess, I still didn't enjoy or see the point of it, and I had reached the stage where I seemed to be improving less with each game rather than more – though as Czernowsky always beat me one way or another, it was difficult to be sure. That was the hardest thing: the thought that in another game, such as tennis, I would probably have had the satisfaction of winning the occasional point or even set. In chess it's all or nothing, and in my case it was nothing. OK, I could take a few pieces off him, but there hadn't been a time when their loss seemed anything other than calculated.

Then one day there came a whisper of hope.

In fact, it wasn't just one day – it was my father's wedding day.

The ceremony took place as planned at Chelsea Registry Office, on a blazing summer's morning. The room was airless, and I felt so hot in my suit that I found it difficult to concentrate on what was being said – which was probably just as well.

If only they could be honest about it, I thought. Why not dispense with the usual vows and simply say, 'I Tony take you Vicky as long as you are reasonably young and sexy and make adequate small talk at dinner with clients', and 'I Vicky take you Tony as long as you can enhance my social status'? It sounds cynical, but as the child of a failed marriage it's difficult to be anything else. I wondered whether my father had believed what he was saying the first time around, and suddenly I felt incredibly lonely and depressed and had to take a deep breath to pull myself together.

Vicky's original idea of a small lunch at the Ritz had been displaced by something more extravagant – a reception for several hundred at Stanley House, further along the King's Road. For oddness, the experience of attending a parent's wedding takes a lot of beating: it's like going to your own funeral, or indeed visiting the house you were brought up in when someone else is living there. I didn't feel angry, just sad and out of place – all the more so because I didn't recognise many of the people present. I assumed they were mainly colleagues of Vicky's and Dad's: you could categorise the males easily enough, because the admen had snappier suits and haircuts than the City types. The women were more problematical: their large hats and short skirts betrayed no particular allegiance.

The bride's skirt (part of a white suit) was shorter than most, while the sloping brim of her hat covered half her face, giving the impression of a standard lamp come to life. Had there been any blushing going on, it would have been invisible, but I was quite sure there wasn't. The only hint of red was supplied by Vicky's startling shoes, which seemed to be what had really caught the imagination of her friends.

'You know what they say – red shoes, no drawers!' exclaimed one corpulent buffer. Vicky scolded him delightedly.

I found Robbie and Sabrina standing by the buffet, looking amused by the whole business.

'Amazing,' said Robbie, gesturing with an asparagus roll. 'It's the revenge of the bourgeoisie. If this mob had turned up at your dad's first wedding they'd have been laughed off the King's Road. But the class struggle continues. Sabrina and I are intercepting vital food supplies. The redistribution of wealth starts here.'

'Show some solidarity,' said Sabrina. 'Try one of those little parcelly things.'

'I'd love to help,' I said, 'but I seem to have lost my appetite.'

'Did you go to the registry office?'

I nodded. 'I don't know why: I suppose I thought that if I turned up and glared in a Hamlet-ish way they might lose their nerve. You didn't miss much.'

'Are any of Vicky's family here?'

'I don't think so. You've heard about her parents, haven't you?'

'Go on,' said Robbie. 'Grass.'

'Apparently they lived in Kenya – her father was a coffee planter – and they were murdered by the Mau-Mau. All very grisly: Vicky won't go into detail, but by some fluke she wasn't in the house at the time, otherwise they might have done her in as well. No, don't say it.'

(Robbie had opened his mouth to speak, but shrugged his shoulders and wolfed a vol-au-vent instead.) 'So there she was, orphaned; some aunt took charge of her, who's now dead, and scrimped and saved to put her through boarding-school. That's her story, anyway. If she wasn't so awful one might feel sorry for her.'

'Those shoes don't look very colonial to me,' said Robbie. 'More like something out of *The Wizard of Oz*.'

'Sebastian!' I looked round and saw Dick Mildmay pushing his way towards us, carrying a brimming glass of champagne. 'God, Robbie, is that you under all those whiskers? Good to see you. *Very* good to see you. Friendly faces around here are as scarce as lawyers inside the pearly gates. I was amazed that Tony invited me – I've hardly spoken to him in years. Still, with business the way it is one can't say no to a free swig of Moët.'

'Hey, Dick,' said Robbie. 'This is Sabrina. Babe, this is Dick Mildmay, otherwise known as Mr Slick.'

'Mr Slick! God, they did use to call me that, didn't they? William Hickey or someone came up with it. I was rather chuffed at the time. So, Robbie, how are you keeping? Still daubing those canvases?'

Robbie nodded. 'That's the way it is for us poor artists – a life sentence. Hard labour all the way, and no remission for good conduct. What about you – still churning out press releases for the enslavers of the masses?'

Mildmay roared with laughter. 'That's right, Robbie. Their lackeys in the media must be fed. God, it's good to come across someone who hasn't changed. I've just seen Ben Shute: do you remember him? Used to work on that underground magazine *Feel* and recite poetry hanging upside down from a branch in Hyde Park; came back from Paris in '68 full of stories of life behind the barricades. Now he owns a property company and recites his poetry in the back of a Rolls-Royce. They say he's about to be had up for fraud.'

'There you are,' said Robbie. 'He's not the great apostate after all, he's simply attacking the system from within.'

'So, Robbie, are you the best man? Are you going to give a speech?'

'Come to think of it, that wouldn't be a bad idea. I could recycle the one I used at Tony's first wedding and forget to change the names. But as I wasn't even invited today, perhaps I shouldn't draw attention to myself.'

'Before I forget, Sebastian, I've got something for you.' Mildmay produced a square envelope from his pocket.

'What is it?' I asked, feeling it. 'A floppy disc?'

'Exactly. One which, I think you'll find, contains the answer to beating our friend Czernowsky at chess.'

I looked at it dubiously, never having had a great deal of faith in computers.

'All you have to do,' he continued, 'is to feed in the moves from your next few games with him. The programme, I am assured by its inventor, will then be able to work out your opponent's basic strategy and predict what move he will make in any given situation.'

'Suppose he has more than one basic strategy?'

'My friend assures me that any ten games will provide all the info the computer needs, however similar or different they may be.'

'That's brilliant,' I said. 'The only trouble is it's me who's going to be playing against him, not the computer. I can't sit there with a terminal on my lap pretending that I'm just doing my annual accounts.'

'No, you can't, which is why you've got to memorise it.'

'Memorise the whole thing?'

'Yes. All you've got to do is make certain key moves, which he will react to in a characteristic manner, and then follow the game plan which the computer has devised for you.'

I was less and less convinced by this. 'Wouldn't it be easier to have a radio receiver hidden in my ear with you at the other end telling me what to do next? I'm sure they did that in a James Bond film.'

'We may yet come to that.' He seemed put out by my lukewarm response. 'In the meantime, you have a lot of homework to do.'

'There's one small objection,' I said. 'It's cheating.'

'Cheating! You make it sound as if this was a fair contest. Is it fair that a beginner like you should be up against someone who was playing before Anatoly Karpov was born? Is it fair that because of some quirk of the law he's sitting there in a house which should rightfully be yours? He's the one who's cheating. And besides, he's always complaining that you don't give him a decent game. Nothing could thrill him more than to find himself with a fight on his hands.'

'He's bound to smell a rat. How could I explain the sudden improvement?'

'Tell him you've taken up transcendental meditation,' said Robbie. 'Tell him you're into Zen and you've like discovered oneness with your pawns.'

'Or chuckle whenever he makes a move,' suggested Sabrina, 'like he's made some really basic mistake. Then he'll think that it's him going to pieces rather than you getting better.'

'I'll think about it,' I said, pocketing the floppy disc.

There was an enormously loud rapping on a nearby table, as if a rash medium had summoned Attila the Hun to a séance. My father was about to make a speech.

'Ladies and gentlemen,' he said, 'I'm not going to give you a great long spiel, because we've got some serious drinking to do.' There was laughter and scattered applause. 'But I would like to thank you all for joining us in our celebrations today. We're particularly grateful to my old friend Zak Mannheim for Concording over from New York, and Nick Patandris for hauling himself away from the fleshpots of Athens, and all of Vicky's colleagues from Barraclough's Paris office who came over last night with, I gather, much revelry. But most of all, of course, I have to thank this gorgeous girl for agreeing to be my wife. It wasn't an easy pitch – in fact, it was one of the hardest I've been involved in – but having won the business, I can only say I'm looking forward to the campaign very much indeed.'

He gave Vicky a kiss, to loud cheers, then held up his hands to ask for silence again.

'Now, if I could ask your indulgence for a couple more minutes, I'd like you to join me in watching a short presentation.'

A curtain was drawn back, a battery of televisions activated, and a sound of native drums thudded through the room. A leopard appeared on the screens, sulking its way through undergrowth; then the film cut to an assortment of frenetic monkeys, dozy lions, stampeding gazelles and yawning hippopotami. 'From the heart of Africa,' declared the voice-over, 'comes a creature of legend. A creature so wild that even the Dark Continent could not hold her. A creature untamed by any man – until now.' Parakeets scarpered through the air, flinging themselves across the screens like bright shrapnel. The scene changed to a beach and the background music to the opening throbs of *Chariots of Fire*. A lion bounced in slow motion across the sand; as the music reached its climax, Vicky leapt from the waves and raced towards him, emitting a roar identical to his own. The lion stopped, turned tail, and hurried back in the direction he had come from. Then my father appeared, looking a little podgy in bright knee-length swimming trunks, and lifted Vicky in his arms. 'Vicky David,' said a fine male voice. 'Conquering virgin Terrytory.'

It seemed to go down a treat with what my father would call the punters. Vicky gave a little shriek, hugging Dad as if she had just won the Eurovision Song Contest. Then, as the applause died away, she stepped forward.

'I know us girls aren't supposed to make speeches at this kind of do,' she said, 'but anyone here who's worked with me knows that I've never taken much notice of that kind of thing.'

It struck me as a strange remark – not because her observation seemed in any way untrue, but because she had chosen to refer specifically to business colleagues rather than friends.

'I'd just like to say that this is a really special day for Tony and me, and we're really thrilled that you're all here to share it with us, because you're all special too. And I'm just sad that my Aunt Pamela, who looked after me when I was a little girl, didn't live to see all this.' There were sympathetic murmurs. 'But anyway, thank you for being here with' (pause, then a giggle) 'my husband and I, because if this was a big pitch for him, it's certainly the most important merger of *my* career. And now we want you to enjoy yourselves. Cheers!' She raised her glass and swallowed the contents.

'Cheers!'

'Oh, and one more thing,' she added. 'You all seem to want to know whether I'm wearing any knickers. The answer is – ask Tony tomorrow!'

Hoots, applause, wolf-whistles. I couldn't take any more. I said goodbye to my companions and then, like the lion, ran a mile.

7.

Kit finds himself standing on a plain. The ground beneath his feet is grey in colour – grey of itself and greyer for the thin layer of dust which covers it. Such texture as it possesses is a shallow roughness shaped in circles, like whispers of craters. This flatness and greyness is all he can see, running ahead and away to either side, towards a horizon which promises more of the same. There are no features here: no rivers, aspiring hills, houses, vegetation. The air is still, settled in a silence deeper than he could have imagined. He moves his foot, but finds the sound utterly absorbed by the dust around it. He wishes to cry out – not from fear, but from curiosity – and tries to do so, only to discover his voice trapped in his throat. He accepts this as a condition of the place.

He looks up to the sky, and the sky is also a grey uniformity, made of clouds of such immensity that their edges are barely discernible. They do not move, but appear to have been there from eternity, moored on adamantine anchors. The line where sky and ground meet in the great distance seems of little consequence.

It is as if his life has been reduced to two dimensions. He feels like a character drawn on a page, caught in the frame of a cartoon, waiting for the artist to allow him movement – or rather, change without movement – into the next situation, or else to offer him a moment's speech. He recognises that he is somewhere where passivity prevails and stasis is the most natural condition. To will himself into action would be a violation.

But as he stares, he begins to be aware of motion – slow and soft in its incipient stage, like a rotating door nudged from stillness. He thinks he hears something now: the gentle friction, he imagines, of the wooden under-edge of a door against the mat beneath it. He closes his eyes to focus on the sensation, but it is touch rather than sound that brushes against him – a touch of wind moving across his face, soothing his temples. It is indefinable as cool or warm; barely definable as wind at all; barely definable as a breeze.

He opens his eyes again and sees that the clouds are moving above him, slipping behind him far faster than a wind as enervated as this could carry them. Looking down, seeking the elusive borderline between sky and ground, he realises that the surface beneath his feet is moving too, with equal swiftness. It is a moment of wild disorientation, like sitting in a train and imagining you are slipping out of the station only to realise with a shock that it is the train beside you that is moving. So with Kit: the clouds move, the ground moves, his feet appear to be on the ground yet he remains still, suspended in space.

The wind mounts. It is a real wind now, pressing hair to his scalp, darting around, blasting, embalming. The clouds seem out of control, like sails torn loose from their rigging, ripping past, whirling in fragments; the ground ripples like a dusty sea, racing giddily beneath his feet. But while all else grows more frantic, the noise in his ears is as subdued as ever, quiet as the breaking of waves against the shore of a different continent.

At last, as his eyes strive to master the dizzy scene, he hears a distant cry, deep, wild: a cry from the abyss echoing through cave after invisible cave, but with an echo which – far from fading away – gathers strength with each reverberation, until it seems to be taken up by a choir of inconceivable magnitude. Kit identifies four distinct words, hurled time and again up to that tormented sky; but their meaning escapes him, like grey dust draining through his grasping fingers, until he is all but deafened. For an instant it comes clear, as if spelt out in the clouds in vast, careering letters, filling all his bewildered mind. 'NO DREAM BUT LIMBO!' the voices thunder. 'NO DREAM BUT LIMBO!'

Then they are gone. The wind drops. Silence falls. Clouds resume their great, lazy patterns. The ground moves with barely detectable motion and breaks into a deep valley.

Below drifting towards him, he sees a great city with wide avenues and vast acres of parkland. It is not like the city where he was born. Sun shines on clean streets, as in an architect's drawing; no tower blocks impede it, no noise of traffic fills the air, no fumes entwine themselves in the breeze. The buildings are elegant, large but not imposing, gathered in crescents and terraces and squares. The people on the pavements, though plentiful, do not amount to a crowd.

They are handsome, cheerful people with time to spare: men and women laughing together at tables outside restaurants or leading skipping children by the hand or reclining in the shade in gardens or next to ornamental lakes. Here a couple walk hand in hand across a Japanese bridge; there a father lifts a baby high on to his shoulders. Their clothes are well-cut, their bodies bold with health. On every corner, it seems, wedding bells ring from churches in shared delight, saluting brides and grooms who seem drunk with happiness.

But there is industry here too. The same man who strolls through the park with his sweetheart can be glimpsed through an open window, head bowed, patiently worrying his thoughts until they run together in a sequence apt for transmission on to the page. In a laboratory, a scientist ponders her instruments, then scribbles on a notepad. An artist decks out his palette, whipping up small, stiff seas of colour. A teacher strides before his blackboard, eyes and voice charged with excitement, gesturing magnificently.

Kit can see that what the writer traces on the page is fine poetry and what the scientist is coaxing to discovery will bring joyful relief to her fellow humans; that the artist with his first few strokes has laid the foundation of his masterpiece while with every word the teacher nurtures greater enthusiasm in rapt pupils. This is a city where all that is striven for can finally be achieved and all that is planted bear fruit. Happiness is the birthright of everyone walking these streets.

It is, moreover, a happiness in which all citizens share. No envious words twist mouths, no bitter looks disfigure faces. Pretensions are unknown. They are delighted with their achievements but not arrogant, humble without being servile. They are full of laughter, at themselves, with each other. And in every garden roses blossom and birds sing and household pets stretch themselves in the sun.

But as Kit moves through the streets – or rather, as the streets move past him – he feels a wind rising and hears again the great cacophony of voices. Looking back over his shoulder at the plain from which he came, he sees the dust that covered it gathered up in a cloud, like a great shroud drawn across the sky and down onto the valley in which this city lies. The light of the sun is blocked; dust falls on every side, making the air so thick that he can barely distinguish the shapes of beautiful houses. The people fall to the ground beneath it, not choking and struggling as one might expect, but submissively, as if overtaken by a great weariness.

The dust buries them like snow. Lovers relinquish each other's hands, families are sundered. Inside the buildings, first floors, then entire rooms are swallowed, filling as relentlessly as the lower chamber of an hourglass. The writer slumps at his desk, his pen clogged and useless. The scientist closes her eyes on instruments that moment by moment surrender precision. Grey camouflages the painter's palette and dries the sticky oils on his canvas. The teacher's marks on the blackboard are eliminated. Roads become indistinguishable from pavements; green parks lose their colour and sheen; the rivers that scampered through the city and nudged its broad bridges begin to grow dark, thick and viscous, until at last they resemble giant earthworms, slithering ever more sluggishly towards underground lairs.

Kit's heart sinks as he witnesses it all. He sees the crevices of the roses filled on every side and hears the heartless wind where once there were songs of blackbirds, ushering in the silence that he knew on the plain above. The people seem to vanish even before they are buried, like ghosts, the radiance of their skin giving way to dullness until it blends with the air and ground alike.

Kit does not know how he can breathe, though breathe he does. Nor does he sink into the dust that gathers beneath his feet. Instead, it seems to buoy him up, carrying him far above the level of the streets, until at last the air clears and he can gaze on a full transformation.

The dust has not buried everything. Just enough remains to suggest what was there before. Buildings retain vague shapes. Church spires, poking up like witches' hats, delineate the street plan of the city. Those wide tableaux must be the commons, those plains punctuated by lustreless trees the parks. The rivers, though, cannot be seen. There is no movement now to betray the lines along which they ran.

Kit weeps to witness it. The sense of loss goes deeper than anything he can understand. But his tears barely smudge the greyness around him, and his sobs fail to carry on the air. Unknown voices, rising from far away, seem to ridicule his sorrow. 'No dream but limbo,' they sing, more softly now. 'No dream but limbo.'

As much through curiosity as anything else, I decided to put the computer programme to the test. I was of course familiar with chessboards designed to play against you; having a computer that actually predicted its opponents' moves was quite another thing. I didn't really believe it could work, and for this reason I had no difficulty in consigning my scruples to a moral deep-freeze. I told myself that even if the programme did prove successful, I could let Czernowsky off the hook by making a deliberate mistake. What I didn't admit was that, having got so close, it might prove extremely difficult to let go.

My opponent was amused by the sight of me meticulously recording our moves. 'How analytical we have become!' he exclaimed. 'You will find, I fear, that analysis is no match for instinct and inspiration; but I'm glad to see that you are taking our challenge so seriously.'

'What are you going to do,' he even asked at another point, 'feed them into a computer?' He laughed so much that I was spared having to make a reply.

Distracted by my hidden agenda, I found myself losing even more emphatically than usual, and it didn't take long to clock up the ten games required. Inputting every move on the Amstrad, however, was a task to fill several evenings. When it was finally accomplished, I went out and bought myself a half-bottle of champagne.

Once the computer had devised the ideal game, the sight of the print-out made me realise I still had a long way to go. How could I possibly learn all these moves by heart? Eventually I realised that the only answer was to play the game over and over until they were stamped on my brain. Even as I did so, I was horribly aware that if I got a single co-ordinate wrong, all this effort would go for nothing.

On the morning of our next meeting I had a sick feeling in my stomach, like the one I used to get at school when we had to recite a poem from memory.

Mr Czernowsky was in a particularly irritable mood. Having let me in, he shuffled off to his high-backed floral armchair without ceremony. The room was horribly stuffy, and I saw the game ahead as a physical ordeal as well as a mental one.

My plan depended on having the opening move. If I drew black, I would have to go through an entire game before I got a second chance, during which the moves prescribed by the computer would inevitably become confused. When I pointed to Czernowsky's right hand and he opened his wrinkled fingers to reveal the palest of pawns, I only just managed to suppress a whoop of triumph.

To impose a pattern on the game, my opening gambit had to be very unorthodox, though not so extraordinary that my opponent would abandon his habitual tactics. That at least was the theory according to Dick Mildmay.

Unfortunately, this meant that I found Czernowsky deliberating far longer than normal at the beginning of a match; and even though my responses were instantaneous, by the end of half an hour we had made fewer than a dozen moves. Miraculously, he had done every-thing he was supposed to; still, I felt myself growing tenser and tenser. After advancing my queen's knight, I excused myself and headed for the downstairs lavatory, where I sank down against the wall and closed my eyes for a minute before taking the print-out from my pocket and studying it anew. Seeing the moves laid out in efficient columns, I felt briefly reassured. As I got to my feet though, I was struck by the ludicrousness of the whole enterprise. How could a machine possibly read a man's mind?

When I returned to the drawing-room, I saw at once that he had diverged from the expected procedure. Instead of countering my knight with a pawn, he had brought his bishop sidling out. I gazed at the board in utter despair. So much for Dick Mildmay's programme. So much for my hopes of ever beating this wretched old man.

I wondered if he had noticed my consternation. Then I realised he wasn't looking at me. He was lying back in the worn armchair, his head at an angle, resting on his left shoulder. If his eyes hadn't been open, I would have thought that he had drifted off to sleep. As it was, it struck me with deep horror that he must be dead.

I knew what I was supposed to do, but since I have some difficulty even in finding my own pulse, I bent down and took his wrist with reluctance. I could feel nothing.

'Mr Czernowsky!' I shouted. 'Mr Czernowsky, are you all right?'

There was no reply. I slapped him half-heartedly on the cheek and loosened his tie, to no avail. I threw a glass of water over him, feeling like a character in a farce; then I realised that I ought to try to give him the kiss of life. Hauling the small body on to the hearthrug, I put my mouth to his.

It was one of the strangest situations I have ever found myself in. To be thrust suddenly into physical intimacy with this man felt like an appalling violation of the distant courtesy that had characterised our relationship. As I pressed against those chapped lips and blew for all I was worth, I tried to sublimate my repulsion by pretending that I was back in first-aid class, training on a plastic dummy.

My pumping and blowing brought no response. Finally I got to my feet, picked up the phone and called for an ambulance.

I couldn't face the idea of sitting in that room with a dead body, so I went out to wait in the garden. I half expected to find it overtaken by the same awestruck silence that now ruled the house, but of course it was business as usual – birds blundering through the undergrowth, a polythene bag in the vegetable garden flapping against the wind, a motorbike puttering up the lane.

I felt in need of a drink, but I could hardly leave a note for the ambulance men saying that I'd gone off to the pub. Nor was I about to start going through a dead man's cupboards in search of alcohol. In fact, I suddenly realised that I couldn't go back into the house on my own. The corpse, which had started simply as a man stripped of life, now assumed a more sinister identity in my mind, as if it had destroyed my adversary and taken his place.

To begin with it scarcely impinged on me that the cottage was now mine. I was worried, indeed, that my Eden would be irreparably tainted by the tragedy that had taken place. Could it be that I was in some way responsible for Czernowsky's death? Had the shock of my unusually sophisticated opening gambit brought on a heart attack?

As well as guilt, there was sorrow. Czernowsky had done nothing to earn my affection; but he had earned my respect. I admired the rigour with which he had lived his life, refusing to subside into an old age which was simply a postponement of the moment that had now come. If the world had been asked for a senior citizen who could be spared easily, he was not an obvious choice.

The ambulance men came, and the police, and went through their routines. It seemed extraordinary that a death from the most natural of natural causes should entail such a rigmarole, but more than two hours elapsed before they told me I could leave. I had no wish to linger; I wanted to start again with the house, to take possession of it unencumbered by Czernowsky's ghost and his stern photographs. Who would remove his effects I didn't know, but I assumed that he had a solicitor who could be tracked down. At any rate, it was not up to me; all I had to do was to show patience.

As I put my hand in my pocket to find my car keys, I felt the stiff folds of the computer print-out, chronicling all the moves that should have been made. Perhaps this was a lesson to arrogant humankind – a rebuke for attempting to sketch the shape of things to come. At a filling station on the way home, I tore the paper into strips and dropped them into the black plastic throat of a rubbish bin, mimicking the stylised figure – the fin-de-siècle common man worthily fulfilling his civic duty – who bent to his chore on the bright red lid.

Stella couldn't make ends meet on the dole; she didn't understand how anybody could. She didn't go out anywhere, except with Clyde, who always paid for her. She didn't eat or drink very much; still, the money seemed to shrivel away like carelessly handled Clingfilm. The heating bill for the flat was the worst thing, but there was no question of cutting down on that: Kit had to be kept warm. And there were all the nappies and clothes he needed: everything was expensive. It was an age since she'd bought something new for herself.

She had taken Kit back to the doctor when there was no change in his condition; the doctor had sent the two of them off to the hospital for 'tests'. The word sounded so innocuous, so like the spelling tests she'd had at school – though she'd never been much good at those – that it was hard to believe that they might reveal something terribly, even fatally wrong with her child; and indeed they revealed nothing. 'It's hard to tell at his stage,' the doctors kept saying. 'We'll just have to wait and see.' They asked her if he had always been a bit withdrawn and mentioned something called autism, but she knew it could be nothing to do with that: it was to do with Ken; and even though she was sure now Ken would never come back to her, she wasn't about to tell anybody what he had done.

She found it hardest lying to Clyde – Clyde, who was kindness personified, always ringing up to see how she and Kit were doing. She wondered why he persisted, since she never gave him encouragement: he still hadn't set foot in the flat, or kissed her except on the cheek – all of which made Ken's jealous rage more painfully ironic. Then she reproached herself for thinking like Ken that he was only interested in one thing, forgetting that some people acted purely out of kindness. Still, she couldn't quite believe that he only wanted to be friends.

She had been with him to his church a few times and found it altogether amazing – quite unlike the quiet, old-fashioned church that her grandparents had taken her to as a child. That of course had been a white church. What a sense of occasion there was at St Jude's! The women in their Sunday best, hats, gloves and all; the children decked out in little suits and shiny shoes; the way they shouted the hymns from the overflowing pews and danced in the aisles! At first she had felt bewildered and embarrassed – she had half expected to be hauled forward to introduce herself and confess her sins before the rest of the congregation – but gradually, reassured by Clyde's smile, she had learnt to relax into it, stop imagining that everyone was staring at her and join in tentatively with the hymns. Not that she really saw the point of it: after all, there was enough to worry about in this life without thinking about what came next; and the whole idea of God seemed hopelessly old-fashioned in an age of television and aeroplanes. She imagined him as a white-haired gentleman in a wing-collar, captured in an indistinct photograph which had been relegated to an attic.

Even going to church cost money. She was never sure how much to put in the collection. On her first visit she had given a pound and spent the rest of the service worrying that Clyde might have noticed and thought her mean, though the truth was she could barely afford even that. The following week she gave half as much. If Clyde's God didn't understand her poverty, she thought defiantly, he wasn't much of a God.

Clyde was always finding ways of helping her. He offered to lend her money, but the suggestion caused so much embarrassment that he was careful not to repeat it. Instead, he brought her little gifts which saved her buying things: a pair of shoes for Kit, or, when the kettle broke, an almost new one which he said was a spare that he had no use for. It all helped. But the worry of money remained.

The job at the hospital had fallen into her lap so easily that she had forgotten how desperate the search for work could be, as if the tribe of hopeless kids hanging around the estate wasn't reminder enough. When she'd met Ken she'd been an assistant in a greengrocer's, but couldn't imagine going back to that. Anyway, she didn't want anything full-time with Kit in his present state.

She decided to try her luck as a cleaner. It didn't pay well, but at least you got cash in hand. She answered some ads and began to build up what Clyde called a client base.

It was a strange experience, being given the run of someone else's house. Sometimes they were there to keep an eye on you, but usually they weren't. It was tempting at first just to wander from room to room, stretching out on beds and sofas and making believe that these things belonged to her; but in reality there was so much work to get through that there was hardly a spare moment. Besides, she couldn't help believing that as soon as she let herself go for an instant, her employer would come home unexpectedly and find her. That was the kind of luck she'd always had.

She gradually became bolder about bringing Kit with her. It began by accident when, after a misunderstanding with the child-minder, she had no choice but to take him to one of the houses she cleaned. The owner – a potter called Anne who lived off Clapham Common, and who thought it very funny when Stella tried to call her by her surname – proved surprisingly sympathetic and, both worried and relieved by the child's unnatural quietness, gave Stella permission to bring him whenever she wished.

As she got to know the people she worked for better and became able to gauge which ones were likely to accede to her request, Stella found she was able to arrange whole days with Kit by her side. Since she would otherwise have had to pay the child-minder nearly as much as she earned herself, the advantages were twofold. Sometimes, though, when she paused in her dusting and looked up to see him staring with disengaged eyes, the despair which fell across her paralysed her, and she could do nothing but hold him and beg whoever there was to beg that he would come back. 'You're as bad as your father,' she whispered half seriously, hugging him with tears in her eyes.

She had heard that listening to music was good for people who had suffered terrible shocks, so wherever she was – as long as there was nobody else around – she would have the radio on. She liked Radio Two best, with all its old pop hits, but she couldn't really believe that Abba or the New Seekers ever healed a wounded psyche, so she searched the airwaves for Radio 3 instead. This seemed a mixed blessing: she could never really get used to opera or strange, scratchy modern string compositions; but she enjoyed grand, thunderous symphonies and quiet, intricate piano pieces in which the notes seemed to knit silence. In between, the calm, posh voice of the BBC announcer spoke as if nothing had changed in the last fifty years and nothing ever would change.

But did these things have any effect on Kit? Impossible to say. Certainly he did not laugh and clap his hands when Bruckner filled the room, but Stella knew that was too much to hope for. All that could be hoped was that, layer by layer, the sounds would line his subconscious until the terror of his father's voice was muffled out.

For her, in the meantime, there was just the daily's life: the drone of the Hoover, splattering of water in the sink, hiss of aerosol polish, wet slap of a mop, soft impact of bedspread on pillow and sudden, alarming, almost-squeak of a duster.

I felt very low when I got back to my flat on the day of Mr Czernowsky's death. I wanted to talk to somebody about it – who, though, would understand my mixed feelings at the passing of this virtual stranger? In the end I rang Robbie, but he was so enthusiastic about the legacy which awaited me that I couldn't begin to explain the downside of it.

To cheer myself up, I rummaged through my collection of videos and found one guaranteed to brighten up the gloomiest of times: *Woodstock*. The first notes of the opening song, 'Long Time Gone', still filled me with an intoxicating mixture of anticipation and contentment. Of course, I wished that I too could have headed down the New York State Freeway to Yatzger's farm; but knowing that future generations could marvel at those few magical days was compensation enough. Marijuana!

The singers are the heroes of *Woodstock:* Richie Havens, strumming as if he were going to snap the strings of his guitar; Joan Baez, her voice as clear and penetrating as an icicle on a breath-freezing night; Alvin Lee, his demonic, hook-nosed face slashed into a pale grin by the footlights. But the film would be nothing without its minor characters: the impossibly awkward television reporter; the raw-voiced clown in a fireman's helmet; an ungainly couple making love in the undergrowth. No matter how often I saw the film, I never tired of their jokes and spaced-out antics.

Guaranteed to brighten up the gloomiest times...Yet on this occasion I found an undertow of sadness in it. Where were they now, I wondered? What had become of the symbolic child born in the middle of it all? How many of them died young like Jimi Hendrix, who closed the show with that wild, mournful version of 'The Star-Spangled Banner'? And who dared to answer the question that acid-eyed John Sebastian asked: 'Could it be that you can't live up to your dreams?'

'We must be in heaven, man,' said the raw-voiced clown, summoning massed groovers to a free breakfast. Then there was only the debris, half-sunk in mud; everyone went away and resumed their lives. It seems to me that Woodstock was the apotheosis of the Sixties: their climax, and in a sense their end.

But, well – good on it. If that event has the power to touch someone like me four decades later, that's something in its favour. Czernowsky wouldn't have been impressed of course; but maybe he had a different take on things at the great free breakfast in the sky. I could see him that moment, sitting on a cloud in the lotus position, with a tie-dyed headband and a fringed jacket, making up for all the things he had missed. Good on you, Mr Czernowsky. Marijuana!

8.

As Kit weeps in Limbo, he notices a movement below him, a stirring, a thrusting through ashes. Somewhere in the loose, choking darkness a sapling has taken root and found the will and nourishment to push towards the half-light. It grows and flourishes before his eyes, projecting broad branches and tortuous roots, unfolding like a conjuror's flower dropped into water. Its leaves are dead on the branches, dry and brittle, like painted paper. Its unknown fruit is wizened and inorganic, like baubles that a stranger's hands have hung by way of decoration. The wind in its leaves seems to speak to him, an unfamiliar language he can somehow understand.

'Here,' it says, 'is the city of lost dreams. Here people came with visions of what their lives might be, but lacking the determination to sustain them. Some were worn down by life and its tragedies; others became forgetful and distracted by mundanity. All failed to recognise the great bounty they had been given; now they have been gathered to a grey sleep.'

Kit looks around him again. As he does so, he becomes aware of a kind of sheen spread across the plain. At first he thinks it nothing but a lucent phenomenon, a growth of phosphorescence, as in an unquiet ocean. Then he discerns, suddenly appearing and vanishing, shapes in the brightness: shapes that might almost be human but fade before they reach definition. Their almost-faces are intent on the ground; they shamble here and there with almost-limbs, flickering through the landscape above the lost city. From time to time one appears to find what it is searching for and throws itself down, motioning as if to dig. But its phantom hands have no purchase on the ashes, difficult enough for solid flesh to grasp; and when it has toiled too long to no avail, it utters a thin cry and writhes on the ground, fading ever more quickly in and out of sight.

At last it clambers to its feet and stands so still that it appears to be its own antithesis, a statue. Gusts of wind come up and gather the ashes around it, dusting over its silhouette. It is left, a sentinel unmourned and unremarked on by its still-searching fellows.

'These are the dreams,' thinks Kit to himself. 'These are the dreams deprived of life by the dreamers who abandoned them.'

The wind rises again, but this time at his back, carrying him on across the landscape. The valley is left behind. He finds himself once more above a plain, dominated by a great building like a mill or warehouse. The wind pauses, depositing him at the entrance, before two broad doors. They are made of oak, studded with iron and joined by a lock of enormous intricacy; yet they open at a touch. He enters.

The courtyard within is empty. Weeds grow between cobblestones and wallflowers prise apart masonry. Doors to stables and store-rooms are rotten and rat-gnawed; a smell of ancient ordure and mildewed hay emanates from them; in their darkness can be glimpsed rusted carcases of machines long idle. The windows, those that have not been broken, are opaque with dust overlaid with cobwebs and further dust. The last flakes of paint are peeling. Plaster has fallen away, leaving ribs of ceilings exposed and piling floors with dry disintegration.

Ahead of Kit is a mossy stone staircase. He begins to climb it, becoming aware of a distant noise like the clamour of birds. As light from the front door recedes below and a faint relenting of darkness above suggests an opening ahead, the sounds begin to resolve themselves into something more nearly resembling human speech.

At the top of the stairs, he enters a vast hall – so vast that one end can barely be seen from the other. The hubbub of voices suggests a room filled to capacity, but the centre is empty. Hundreds, if not thousands, of people here are spread out along walls, their backs to Kit, staring at the huge, many windows. Kit can gather shards of conversation, but it is beyond him to piece them into a coherent whole. What he hears is not dialogue so much as indications of dialogue:

'I heard…'

'He said that…'

'He told me…'

'I saw…'

'I read…'

'I was watching…'

Following the people's gaze, Kit looks through the enormous windows. He finds that even where they are set side by side the view from each is quite different.

Through the first he sees, to his amazement, another room

thronged with people: it is of the same lay-out and dimensions as the hall in which he stands, so that for the first instant it is like gazing into a mirror; but the contents and people in it are quite different. Instead of bare boards the room boasts an opulent carpet, while the walls are transformed by gold-framed paintings and extravagant tapestries; beautiful and ingenious furniture of mahogany and sandalwood, carved and inlaid; delicate boxes of pearl and lapis lazuli; statues of marble and bronze; gold dishes and intricate vases – all crowd the glass. Among them figures of great elegance move like horses in a parade ring. Expensively dressed, decked in jewellery, with carved hair, they mimic the action of a kaleidoscope, forming patterns, breaking apart and reforming in drifts of colour. Every so often one of them seems to shine too intensely and of a sudden catch fire, shrivelling into bright air. Those around look momentarily embarrassed, then resume their conversation. Those who watch marvel and cheer.

Moving to the next window, Kit gazes on a beach where a party of men labours to save a ship which has foundered in a storm. Some, hauling on ropes, strive to pull it clear of the rocks; others in small boats battle to bring off the crew; others still plunge into the water and swim towards desperate figures floundering in dark currents. One man, more muscular and handsome than the rest, regains the shore with a hysterical child in his arms and lays her gently on the sand. Exhausted, he sinks down beside a fire of driftwood and spreads his arms to dry his shirt in the heat. Helpers bring blankets and a bowl of soup. Although others carry on as frantically as before, this one man, resting and drinking, holds the spectators' interest. A glow of more than firelight seems to descend on him, setting him apart from the rest, while his fellow rescuers fade into darkness.

Kit turns to a third window and sees a land mutilated by war and famine. Families in rags crouch beside the ruins of a wall, seeking shade from a skeleton tree. Nearby, a dry riverbed forms a grim repository for the bodies of old and young, molested by flies. A snake entwines itself nonchalantly about a child's skinny limb. Soldiers parade across the scene, their shiny weapons passports to a yet more primitive world. Refugees, most blinded with misery, watch them with whatever fear exhaustion can muster; a shot is fired at random, a child falls dead. Kit turns away, but the figures gathered at the window still stare, as hungry for these strangers' tears as the riverbed is for rain.

Kit moves to a fourth window. It presents a happier scene: a park filled with children. Some are infants as he was on earth, sleeping and crawling and testing their unfirm limbs; some are older, enjoying their first games together, engrossed by building blocks and soft toys. Then there are those eager for adolescence and adulthood, deep in books, experimenting with simple machines, striving to outdo each other in study and sport. Here more than at any of the other windows, the spectators appear to be all-absorbed. Glancing back and forth between watchers and watched, Kit begins to detect a resemblance between the two; then he realises that these are parents of the children in the park. What strikes him above all is that the sounds they are making are identical to those of their offspring: they echo their wails, shouts, mutterings, laughter.

Kit realises too what all these groups of spectators at their various windows have in common. It is not the different sights which define them, but the act of watching. 'These are the people,' he thinks, 'who have led their lives at second-hand: who, rather than do, find excitement in things done by others. Discontented with their circumstances, they gloat over the possessions of the rich; lacking the stomach for adventure, they construct heroes wherever they can find them; no longer moved by the misery of those around them, they gorge themselves on high tragedy; making no headway in their own lives, they pin all their hopes upon their sons and daughters.'

He begins to weep again. Leaving the crowds of people as rapt as ever, he descends the stone staircase.

I waited for some weeks after Mr Czernowsky's death before going to talk to my father about the cottage. This was partly out of some ill-defined respect for the dead and partly to allow time for the legal side of things to be sorted out. I was in a positive mood after a morning spent developing my latest mushroom pictures, which I hugged proudly to my chest in an expensive portfolio. Sunlight zinged off the chrome-girdled building where Terry Bowie Brady Montrachet-Lefèvre had its headquarters. I was almost looking forward to my meeting with Dad.

It was the first time that I had been to TBBML House – the company had recently moved to Soho from Victoria – so my visit was of some interest to the voluptuous receptionist. Mr Terry, she said, was just finishing a meeting. Would I care to wait in his office?

It was a room remarkable only for its size. The chrome that featured prodigally on the exterior had insinuated itself here too, propping up desk and chairs in gleaming zigzags and framing the posters that gave a visual résumé of my father's career. On a low, glass-topped table, glossy magazines from three continents were laid out as carefully as a game of solitaire. A portrait of Vicky in an expensive, boring green-leather frame was propped in one corner of the window sill.

Dad's meeting dragged on, and my mood began to sag. I picked up *Rolling Stone* and *Hong Kong Tatler*, but the content barely repaid the effort of turning pages. I made a phone call. I went to the gents.

When I returned, Dad was sitting at his desk going through my portfolio. I wasn't sure whether to be flattered or angry and braced myself for a sarcastic put-down. I was astonished when he said, 'These are really interesting.'

'Thanks,' was all I could manage.

'How do you get these effects?'

'Trade secret.'

'No, tell me.'

'I impregnate the pages with hallucinogens from the mushrooms. You absorb them through your fingertips and start tripping.'

He laughed. 'OK, I'll mind my own business. Did they offer you some coffee?'

'Yes, but I didn't want any.'

'Very wise. We've just got the account for a new instant blend from Holland, so we've all got to drink it. Tastes filthy. So tell me, to what do I owe the pleasure of this visit?'

'I've come to talk about the cottage.'

'Right,' he said, swivelling his chair and staring out of the window. 'Right. Frederick Czernowsky, R.I.P.'

'I'd like to move in as soon as possible, so I wondered if we could get going on the paperwork.'

'Paperwork. Yes.' He seemed absorbed by the unequivocally dull brickwork of the building opposite. 'You realise, of course that half of the cottage belongs to your mother. You have to bear that in mind.'

'Dad, I realise that, and you can leave me to sort it out. Unless she's had enough of Turkey and wants to come back and live in it, I don't see that there's a problem.'

'She'll probably want some money for it. I don't think she's exactly rolling.'

'Well, of course. The idea is to pay her half the market value.'

'And how are you going to do that?'

'I'm going to sell my flat. It should fetch about twice what I paid for it, so I can pay off the mortgage and give Mum the difference. If that isn't enough, I'll take out another mortgage.'

'I see,' he said. 'I'm afraid there's a problem, though, as far as Vicky and I are concerned. We really need a bigger place, and we need to sell the cottage to pay for it.'

Suddenly everything in the room came into much sharper focus. My father's desk seemed to move towards me on skeleton legs; the framed posters leered like holograms.

'Dad,' I said. 'You promised. You said the cottage would be mine.'

'I don't think I ever put it quite as definitely as that. It's quite true that I *hoped* to hand my share over to you. But circumstances change. I have to think of Vicky. It wouldn't be fair to keep her cooped up in that little house.'

'Fair!' I couldn't remember when I had last shouted at someone, but I shouted now. 'What about me? That "little" house has four bedrooms. And don't tell me that you're not both earning a fortune.'

'I'm certainly not earning a fortune,' he said. 'In case it has entirely escaped your notice, times are hard in the advertising industry. Vicky is of course doing very well, but if we decide to have children we can no longer rely on her salary. We are not in any position to give away tens of thousands of pounds.'

'Czernowsky could have lived another twenty years. You would have managed then. I'm simply asking you to give me what you promised me when it was of no use to either of us.'

'As I said, I don't think I gave you anything that amounted to a promise.' He finally looked me in the eye. 'I'm sorry if you got the wrong impression.'

'I think the wrong impression is about all you ever have given me,' I said bitterly. 'For some reason I imagined that fathers were supposed to treat their sons with affection rather than as clients to be screwed if they don't read the small print. It's not as if you've showered me with presents and love and concern.'

That did it. He leapt to his feet and began yelling like a dyspeptic preacher. 'And *I* imagined that sons were supposed to show their fathers a little respect. But oh no; you've ignored all the advice I've ever given you, and look where it's got you. If you'd followed up the opportunities I handed you, you wouldn't have to come here scrounging. You've always wanted something for nothing; now you're asking for a free house so that you can sit on your backside doing damn all. You're an ungrateful little sod, and if Vicky and I have children like you, I might as well give up.'

Although I was aware of the enormous noise he was making, I

found myself surprisingly detached from this tirade, as if it were not directed against me at all. I remember wondering whether I had ever seen him quite so red in the face and whether I would ever be able to forgive him for these words.

I tried to speak calmly, but I was aware that my voice was shaking. 'I think you should consider what you're doing very carefully. I think you should consider the full consequences. If you sell that cottage, our relationship is at an end. Full stop.'

He looked as if he was about to start shouting again, but instead sank back in his chair. 'Don't patronise me, Sebastian. Get out.'

As I travelled down in the lift, I wondered at how my father had managed to present himself as the injured party. It was a long time since I had imagined him as a moral arbiter; but I couldn't think of a situation in which he had so wilfully adopted a false position. I had in effect been forced into a role reversal – myself playing the rebuking adult, he the errant child.

Adulthood, as I keep telling myself, is about accepting responsibility – not because you believe you are ready for it, but because you have come to realise how little other people can be relied on. I can remember as a child watching student demonstrations on television and thinking how impossibly mature those eighteen-year-olds seemed; when I became one myself, I realised with a shock that they were anything but – and so it continued. It should have been clear to me from quite early in my schooldays that the world was in a mess, and few of those who ran it were qualified to sort things out; but you tend to give your elders the benefit of the doubt. As time goes by, you find yourself less and less able to do that. Then, on a day like this day, you realise you can rely on no one but yourself.

It occurred to me to go and squat at Harbury, but that was only a short-term solution. A more satisfactory one lay with my mother. Dad couldn't do anything about the cottage without her agreement, and if she refused to sell to the same person as him, he was stuck. The time had come to renew contact.

Stella had a new employer. Anne the potter had told her of a friend who was looking for someone to do two hours' cleaning a week and an hour's ironing. He was, Anne said, a reasonably tidy person by nature, so it wouldn't be as bad as dealing with some bachelors' flats. Stella was glad of the extra work and delighted that Anna was sufficiently pleased with her to recommend her to someone else. It was the first time that this had happened since she had started her new profession.

The man seemed nice enough: youngish, not bad-looking, slightly nervous, obviously not used to giving orders to people. In fact Stella preferred working for men (apart from the embarrassment of what she might come across in the bedroom), because they only had a vague idea of what they wanted and left her to get on with it. Some of the women insisted on guiding her through every nook and cranny of their houses. It wasn't that she worked less hard for men, merely that she didn't feel under such pressure.

The flat in question was on the second floor of a grimy-bricked terraced house. There was a bicycle in the communal hall and a pile of junk mail which someone kept tidy but never got around to throwing out. The stairs weren't her responsibility, but she occasionally Hoovered them just the same. It was one of those awkward conversions which left the bathroom adrift – around the corner and on a different level to everything else – and the kitchen plunging alarmingly away from the sitting-room. The furniture seemed slightly too big for the space: Stella often found it awkward to manoeuvre her way round.

The most attractive room was the bedroom, which was hung and carpeted with elaborate, colourful oriental fabrics, giving it the feel of a fortune-teller's booth. Some of the rugs were a bit shabby, as were many of the clothes in the built-in wardrobe, and Stella couldn't understand why someone who could obviously afford new things should surround himself with tat. The same was true of the kitchen, which was full of old plates and cups, none of them amounting to anything like a set: they seemed to belong on a second-hand stall in a street market. Not that their owner left any washing-up for her to do. The only actual mess was on the kitchen table, every available inch of which was covered in letters and documents, envelopes and magazines. He had asked her not even to try to tidy it up.

It wasn't clear what he did for a living, but she knew that he didn't have an ordinary office job because he had insisted that she come in the afternoon rather than the morning: he sometimes worked late and needed to sleep the following day. She thought that he must be quite an efficient worker, because unlike many of the other people she worked for he never forgot to leave money for her or to buy bleach, floor-cleaner or any of the other things she told him she needed.

There wasn't any evidence of a girlfriend or close relatives – not a single family portrait on the mantelpiece. There were a couple of big photographic collages, like the ones she saw in a lot of houses showing the owners skiing or sitting on a beach or wearing party hats around a dinner table; only these were more serious, the one in the bathroom showing beautiful landscapes and the one in the kitchen a whole range of people, from shopkeepers to film stars. She often took a break to stare at them. One in particular she kept returning to: it showed an old black man sitting with a torn straw hat in his hand on the steps of a veranda, grinning as if he'd never had his picture taken before. There was something peculiarly attractive about that face – a mix of wisdom, innocence and good humour – which made his obvious poverty irrelevant. It reminded her of Clyde. She wanted to borrow it and show it to him, imagining him exclaiming that by some incredible coincidence it was one of his relatives. But of course her employer would miss it, and so she had to make do with admiring it and giving it the mental label, 'Clyde's grandfather'.

There were other intriguing photos in the flat, neatly framed and hung along the wall as if in a gallery: still lives and intense portraits, always in black and white. Most conspicuous of all was a grainy study of a singer caught in a spotlight, eyes closed in deep concentration, microphone tipped lightly towards her lips. Stella didn't recognise her until she read the inscription in a corner: 'To Sebastian, with best wishes from Dusty Springfield.'

9.

Kit journeys on through the grey, twilight world. When the plain has been borne past him, he finds himself lifted over steep mountains – so steep that he thinks the sun would struggle to rise above them, if ever the sun came to that dull land. Their shapes excite a vague memory, but there is no comparison with the mountains of heaven. To Kit, carried upwards through passes and ravines, the landscape seems like a crude charcoal scrawl.

When he attains the summit, a fitting sense of bathos awaits him. No panorama of rivers and valleys stretches before him, no sharp descent to take his breath away. Instead, a plateau as tedious as the plain he has left behind. The horizon is as unbeckoning as before.

But in the end something pierces the monotony. Coming closer, Kit sees what seems to be a new and vigorous community. On the edge of a forest, teams of men are busily engaged in building houses. The trees beside them are felled, sawn, stripped of bark; foundations are dug deep in the earth; frames are raised, beams thrown across them and planks nailed in place. The men work with a will, with joy, singing together to the rhythm of hammer and saw.

Though each of the houses is different in design, the effect is harmonious. Some are larger than others, some more elaborate, but shape and size are of less consequence than the spirit in which they are built. The enthusiasm is effulgent.

Within the forest are other men who want no part in this. Their dwellings are uninviting – bare caves, makeshift shelters – but rather than join the builders at work they gather to sit by a fire, burning timber the house-makers have discarded. Their talk is not the happy talk of the carefree and idle, but a low grumbling which threatens to erupt in furious confrontation.

From time to time, a handful of them walk to the forest's edge. They stand watching the builders at work, arms folded, eyes insolent. They begin to make sarcastic remarks, damning the design and workmanship. One ridicules the hanging of a door, another the whole edifice. Then they start to abuse the builders, who do their best to ignore them; but a few, dispirited, pause in their tasks, questioning their own judgement.

The hour comes for the workmen to rest. They lay aside their tools and stretch out in their houses to sleep. While they are off guard, the men from the forest come closer, carrying sledgehammers and flaming torches lit from their camp fire. They attack the finished and unfinished buildings, smashing the doors and walls and roofs or setting them ablaze. Many of the workmen fight to defend what they have built, but some take fright and abandon the struggle, and others perish inside their burning houses.

Kit watches with a heavy heart. He knows the language of this tenebrous world now: he recognises that here is a place where those incapable of dreaming themselves find a savage consolation in destroying the dreams of others. But he feels as helpless as he did in the first months of infancy. He can only watch. And as he watches, the wind rises again and bears him onwards.

The last thing I expected was for my father to ring up a few days after our confrontation and offer to smoke the peace pipe. That however is exactly what he did. He said that we had both got carried away and now that we had had a chance to cool off, why didn't we get together for lunch – with Vicky – and see if we couldn't come to some sort of compromise? Reluctant to believe that he'd had a change of heart, but more reluctant to exclude the smallest possibility of reconciliation, I agreed to meet them the following week at a hip new Italian place a couple of streets from his office.

It was the kind of restaurant whose waiters wore waistcoats in bright primitivist designs and the different kinds of mineral water took half an hour to explain. I had finally settled for some high-iron Latvian fizz when I spotted the newlyweds out of the corner of my eye, crossing the road hand in hand.

Vicky was wearing a particularly severe suit and, in spite of the grey day, dark glasses. I had to kiss her, though never was a cheek so reluctantly offered or franked. She refused the Latvian spa water – flatly, you might say – in favour of a still Scottish variety and scanned the menu with a frown, as if checking the latest prices from Wall Street.

'The bruschetta is a good starter,' said my father. 'So is the celeriac soup.'

'I think I'll have anchovy crostini,' said Vicky, dropping her menu and checking the room for familiar faces, 'followed by the calf's liver.'

I asked for Caesar salad and lemon sole and immediately regretted both choices.

'Good place this, don't you think?' said Dad. 'Lots of buzz.'

Buzz was an understatement. The acoustics seemed to snatch words from your mouth and fling them across the room like Jonty Rhodes attempting a run-out, bringing back a babble of strangers in their place. A worse spot for serious discussion was unimaginable.

'I wish that waiter would get a move on,' said Vicky. 'If any of our servants in Africa had been that hopeless, my father would have kicked them out on the spot.'

'No shortage of staff, then?' I said.

She knew I was winding her up, but decided to ignore it. I wondered why – and, for the thousandth time, why I had been summoned to this lunch. They must want something out of me. What?

'No,' she replied. 'My father would tell the butler that he needed a new gardener or whatever, and the next day there'd be twelve men lined up after breakfast hoping for the job.'

The word 'butler' suggested a degree of refinement that I had not hitherto associated with Vicky's childhood. I saw her seated at a cane table in a muslin dress and white gloves while a black flunky in a powdered wig and knee breeches served her tea and macaroons, a lion cub rolling playfully at her feet. I envisaged a respectful groom holding her pony's head as she dismounted after a day spent visiting the headmen of local villages with her father; and, finally, her parents seated on the veranda in evening dress while the Mau Mau watched with cold eyes from bushes lush with tropical blooms.

We didn't get on to the subject of the cottage until the second course. Vicky recounted the indiscreet carryings-on of her firm's personnel manager, while Dad essayed some light remarks on the future of the monarchy. But if they were hoping that a diet of Caesar salad, good wine and pleasantries would make me more tractable, they were wrong, even though the nature of my father's initiative caught me completely unawares.

'How's your mushroom book coming along?' he asked.

'Very well, thanks.'

This was not strictly true. I had somehow allowed a string of trifling jobs for magazines to come between me and the book. I'd also been preoccupied by the cottage to an extent which left me unable to concentrate on anything else.

Dad harried a stray wedge of cauliflower with his fork. 'As far as the cottage is concerned, Vicky and I have been thinking. As I told you, we're not in a position to give away our assets. On the other hand, I'm prepared to concede that you had certain expectations which I may have inadvertently encouraged.

'What we have in mind is a kind of quid pro quo. To be quite frank, there's something that you can do for me. We're pitching for a big supermarket account: the company concerned is particularly keen to push its fresh food, and I think those mushroom photographs of yours could be exactly the kind of thing we're looking for.'

There was no need to spell it out, but Vicky did anyway. 'If you agree to do the photographs for the campaign, and the pitch is successful, then you'll receive our share of the cottage. Of course it's a payment way, way over the odds, but it's a gesture towards family harmony that I'm prepared to go along with it.'

I was flabbergasted. The account must have been mega for them to make this kind of offer; in fact, I guessed, the whole future of Dad's agency must have depended on it. To think that I was to be the saviour of Terry Bowie Brady Montrachet-Lefèvre – I, the no-good, priggish son with my preciously arty photographs! It must have cost Dad an awful lot to come to that conclusion. The irony of the situation fizzed around me like the bubbles in my mineral water.

But I didn't feel triumphant, or even flattered. I felt incensed that what was mine by right was being dangled in front of me as a bribe.

'It would be a fantastic campaign,' my father added, interpreting my stunned silence as an encouraging sign. 'Your pictures in every colour supplement, and on hoardings all over the country. It would be the making of you.'

I got to my feet. 'No way,' I said. 'No *way*.'

'Think about it,' Dad called after me as I headed for the stairs.

Reaching them, I glimpsed him and Vicky in one of the mirrors which threw a belt of clear light around the walls. She looked angry; he looked surprisingly pleased with himself, as if this were exactly what he had expected. 'Don't worry, darling,' I could imagine him saying, 'he'll come around to the idea.'

Worst of all was the suspicion that he might be right.

'Heavy,' said Robbie. 'Very heavy. And very typical of your old man. You want to know how he got to the top in advertising? That's how.'

'You must be very tempted,' said Sabrina.

'Well, yes,' I said. 'Being offered the thing I want most in the world in return for a little bit of hypocrisy? I think that amounts to a pretty good case study in temptation.'

'Just so you know,' she said, 'I'm neutral in all this. Yes, the advertisements would be great for the book, there's no doubt about that. But if it's something you really don't want to do, then I'm happy for you not to. Anyway, the mere fact that your father is so excited about the pictures shows we're on to a winner.'

It was sweet of her, but it didn't make my dilemma any easier.

'I used to imagine,' I said, 'that when this kind of decision had to be made it would be clear-cut; but of course it never is. If I say no, I'll not only lose all hope of getting the cottage, but I could be shutting the door on the biggest opportunity of my career – which is pretty hard when your name means nothing except to a handful of art directors on low-circulation magazines. I've started telling myself that I wouldn't be debasing my art, I'd be elevating advertising to the status of art.'

'Yeah,' said Robbie, 'but you ask your dad what he's been doing for the last thirty years, and he'll tell you exactly that. You want to know about selling out? I've watched most of my generation do it – and how many of them see it that way? Virtually none. It's not like they say, "Look at me, I traded in my dreams for a Porsche" – it's "Oh, we were so naïve". Well, man, I'm still naïve, but at least I'm happy.'

He put his hand over Sabrina's, and they grinned at each other. The houseboat swayed slightly as a motor launch droned past, V-ing the water into a wake.

'I can't say that Dad looked exactly miserable today. In fact, when he showed up with the new Mrs Terry he looked like the Cheshire cat who'd got the double cream.'

'Give them a couple of years,' said Robbie. 'She'll have her claws in him as deep as a man-eating tiger. You know what all this reminds me of? Milton's idea of devils being tortured by their absence from God and only finding relief in dragging others down. You go along the same road as your dad, and it'll make it that much easier for him to live in his skin.'

'Of course, there's no guarantee that my pictures would be chosen for the campaign anyway. Then I'd lose on every count: no cottage, no nationwide recognition, no self-respect.'

'Cheer up, Silver Surfer – there's got to be an alternative solution. All that's needed is a little lateral thinking.'

'I suppose I could murder Dad and hope that he's left the cottage to me in his will. But I might just be doing Vicky a favour.'

'What I had in mind was something a little less extreme.'

'Like?'

'Seeing where your mother stands in all this.'

'I've thought of that. In fact, I've been trying to get hold of her for the last two weeks, but her number seems permanently engaged. When I finally got through yesterday, there was a guy at the other end who didn't speak a word of English. I'll have to write.'

I explained my plan to buy her share of the cottage. 'The problem is,' I concluded, 'it could take me months to sell the flat. If she's very hard up, and Dad and Vicky can come up with the money faster than I can, she might sell to them. And suppose she did sell to me: what would that leave me with? Half a cottage that I might or might not be able to occupy.'

'Possession is nine-tenths of the law,' said Sabrina. 'If you can stop your father and stepmother selling to anyone else, then you've won most of the battle.'

'Dad can be pretty bloody-minded; and now that he's got that woman in tow, we're talking about exponential growth.'

'I've got to hit the road,' said my uncle. 'There's some guy over from Houston wants to take a look at my work in progress. But if I were you, I'd get on a plane right now to the heart of the Ottoman empire. And give your mother my love.'

'I don't know what to do about him,' said Stella. 'I swear to God I don't. The doctors can't find nothing wrong with him, and I don't like to go on bothering them. Every time I goes to the health centre I sees them looking at me, thinking, "Here's that poor loony again thinks there's something the matter with her baby. She's the one what wants her head looking at".'

'Now, come on,' said Clyde. 'You know it's not like that. They think you're a concerned mother, that's all, trying to do the best for her kid. Anyone can see that there's something up with him, that he's had a little shock – '

'What do you mean, a little shock?' said Stella defensively. Could he have guessed what had really happened?

'I mean a little shock like you get when you fall out of a pram. I don't think even adults like you and me would enjoy that too much.'

'No,' said Stella. 'I suppose.'

'What we could do,' he added, 'is go and see Mother Amelia.'

Although Clyde did his best to explain, Stella couldn't quite work out who or what Mother Amelia was. She was like a nun, he said, only she was married with a family; or a counsellor – but no, not a psychiatrist: there was no need to worry about that. She was a wise woman, and a holy one, and Clyde knew lots of people who had been to see her in times of trouble.

Stella agreed to go because she was desperate enough to try anything, but she had misgivings. Although Clyde was the most Christian person she knew – or seemed to be – she kept thinking about this film she'd seen set in the Caribbean. What was it called? *I Walked With A Zombie?* Something like that. Anyway, she kept thinking that Mother Amelia must somehow be mixed up with voodoo and all that: perhaps she would ask for Stella's soul in return for saving Kit. Stella wondered whether she would give it to her.

By the time of the visit, Stella had reached such a pitch of apprehension that the reality was something of a disappointment. Mother Amelia's house in Peckham wasn't hung with masks or spears or shrunken heads, but with pictures of Jesus and the Virgin Mary in gold-painted plastic frames, embellished with red or silver tinsel. The door was opened not by a silent, spectral man with glazed eyes but a cool teenage boy in a baseball cap, and there was every appearance of a normal family life being carried on in unseen rooms – the smell of chips, scraping of chairs on floorboards, tinny reverberation of a television, laughter. Of course that sort of thing could probably be arranged easily enough if you knew the right spells; but there was something so overwhelmingly reassuring about Mother Amelia herself that Stella's anxiety about black magic was gone in an instant.

She was a small woman with enormous spectacles and an equally enormous smile. She wore a bright purple scarf around her head, which concealed the colour of her hair and exacerbated the already difficult task of guessing how old she was – Stella estimated fifty, but was afterwards assured by Clyde that she was at least twenty years short of the mark. Mother Amelia's only visible disability, apart from short sight, was a slight crook in her back, which created the impression of a benign tortoise.

She led the way down a hall to what she called her parlour – a cramped, dimly lit room with more than its share of holy pictures. She invited Stella to take a seat in a deep chair with worn arms; Stella lowered herself into it warily, taking Kit on her knee, while Clyde hesitated in the doorway. Mother Amelia shooed him away.

'We don't need you, Clyde. You go and sit in the kitchen with Lee and talk men's nonsense with him. Now, child,' she said to Stella once he had retreated, 'you tell me everything that's wrong.'

Stella went through her speech about Kit's supposed accident in the pram. Though well-rehearsed by now, it seemed to her unconvincing in a way that it hadn't when told to Clyde or the doctors. With them, she had almost come to believe the story herself; under Mother Amelia's gaze she felt her voice weakening and her heart unwilling to complete the story. She brought it to a conclusion feeling guilty and exposed.

Mother Amelia frowned. 'If you don't tell me the truth, there's nothing I can do to help you. You can go now, or you can start again.' There was no anger in her voice, but the rebuke made Stella feel like a child being told off by her grandmother. She thought briefly about going and how she would explain it to Clyde. Then she started again.

'Good,' said Mother Amelia once she had finished. 'Now we know what we are dealing with. Have you told any of this to Clyde?'

'No,' said Stella. She was going to add that he was just a friend and that the state of her relationship with Ken wasn't his concern but then realised that wouldn't wash either.

'Don't worry, I won't tell him. I don't believe in deceiving people, but I also don't believe in saying things that will only hurt them. I hope the time will come when you feel able to tell him yourself. With God's help, it will. Now, give me the child.'

Mother Amelia held out her arms. Stella hesitated, then lifted Kit and handed him to her. He made no protest. The woman set him on her knee and began to rock him gently from side to side, staring into his face.

'Do you love Clyde?' she asked.

'I don't know,' said Stella, caught off guard. 'Honest,' she added, fearing that she was about to be thrown out. 'I ain't really thought about it.'

'Don't you think it's about time that you did?'

'I suppose so.' The truth was that she didn't want to. Clyde was a comforting presence she was reluctant to lose, by either elevating him to a closer relationship or turning him down. Her feelings about Ken were complicated enough without adding Clyde to the equation.

'I'm not going to tell you what you should feel for him,' said Mother Amelia. 'He didn't ask me to, and he'd be embarrassed if he thought I'd taken the job on myself. But I don't think you're being fair on him right now. You know that, don't you?'

'Yes,' said Stella with a heavy heart. Goodness knew why she'd thought she could just let things drift along, but she had.

'You may think I'm just a nosy old woman,' Mother Amelia continued, 'and that this has nothing to do with your baby. But it does. Now, let's take a good look at him.'

She stopped rocking Kit and turned him on her knee so that they were staring into each other's eyes. They sat silently like that for so long that Stella found herself falling half asleep and came to with a jerk when Mother Amelia spoke again.

'The child is far away from here,' she said. 'He is with God. I have seen it before, though never quite like this. We all have the desire to go back to where we came from, but in him it is very, very strong. He has not found this world a welcoming place.

'Whether he will return to us or when, I don't know. The important thing is to make a secure home for him here. You give Kit a lot of love, I can see that; but a child needs a father too, and though Kit has been rejected by his own father Clyde can give him affection enough to compensate. Now mind, I'm not saying that you should join together with Clyde simply for the sake of your little boy: that would be foolish. But I want you to think about him seriously because I know he loves you, and I think it is in your heart to love him. In the meantime, child, we must watch and pray.'

Stella had felt soothed by Mother Amelia's words, but now she was disappointed. 'You mean there ain't nothing you can do for him, and we just got to carry on like before? Ain't you got no cures?'

Mother Amelia smiled. 'For this there is no cure stronger than the power of prayer. Believe me.'

She reached out and patted Stella on the cheek. It was a completely unexpected gesture, and for a moment Stella again felt like a child in the presence of a grandparent. But this time it was the comfortable presence of someone who knew far more about life than her.

'Sorry,' she said, smiling back. 'Thanks.'

Clyde drove her back to her flat.

'She's a wonderful woman, isn't she, Mother Amelia?' he said.

Stella nodded.

'What did she say to you?'

'That Kit was with God. That he might come back to us. She wasn't sure. A lot of things.'

'It's OK,' he said gently. 'You don't have to tell me.'

'I'd like to tell you. But... I can't explain, see. I'm sorry. It's all so difficult.'

'It's *OK*,' he said. 'Really.'

When they arrived he helped her and Kit out of the car as usual. Stella hesitated. 'Fancy coming up?' she said.

He tried to hide his surprise. 'Yes,' he said, with a quiet smile. 'That would be nice. I'll just park the car.'

She watched anxiously as he manoeuvred the Vauxhall into a space and sauntered back to her. Was she doing the right thing?

'Don't tell me, it's the lift operator's night off,' he said as he pushed the button for her. 'I have the same problem at the Clyde Tower. You just can't get staff to work the hours they used to.'

Stella laughed. She liked him best when he was being funny: he always knew how to break the tension. Even so, she was glad that there was no one in the corridor to observe them when they emerged on the eighth floor.

'Here we are,' she said, opening her front door. 'It ain't much.'

'Not much!' exclaimed Clyde. 'It's a palace! Compact flat, conveniently located for central London, with unparalleled views of one the capital's most fashionable estates; fully furnished reception area with period fireplace and original features; en suite fitted kitchen featuring hi-tech refrigerator, toaster and electric cooker, well stocked with cornflakes; extensive play facilities for infants; what more could you want? I'll take it. Will £100,000 do as a deposit?'

'No,' she said. 'But it might buy you a cup of tea.'

'Milk's extra, I suppose?'

'That's right. Keep an eye on Kit, will you?'

She put the kettle on to boil and, while she was waiting for it, glanced through the doorway at Clyde and her baby. Clyde had picked up a box of tissues and was sitting on the floor next to Kit, flying it backwards and forwards, up and down in front of Kit's face like an aeroplane. Kit's response was minimal as it always was these days, but Clyde showed no sign of losing patience, smiling and weaving his arm around and making ridiculous noises. If only Kit would come back, she thought, what fun they could all have together!

What had Mother Amelia meant by Kit being with God? It was one of those things which seemed to make sense at the time but you couldn't quite explain afterwards. She dropped the teabags into the pot and watched them swell slowly, buoyed plumply upwards. Then she put the cups and milk and half a packet of biscuits on a tray and carried them through.

'How delicious,' said Clyde. 'I haven't tasted tea like this since I visited the Maharajah of Bombay at his house in the jungle. The table was a stuffed tiger standing on all fours. Kit would have enjoyed riding it. Perhaps the zoo can lend us one.'

Stella said nothing, so he went on. 'Did you know that I used to work at London Zoo? I was an assistant keeper looking after the giraffes. It was the only time I've come across racial discrimination that worked in my favour. Trouble with those giraffes was they never looked where they were going – they were so busy looking out for delicious trees to eat, though of course there weren't any, that they didn't tend to notice all us little fellows running around their kneecaps. You had to watch out that you didn't get your toes trodden on. Oh, but they were beautiful animals!'

Stella remained silent. Clyde looked at her anxiously. 'You all right?' he asked. 'Mother Amelia didn't upset you, did she?'

She shook her head. 'There's something I got to tell you though.' She took a deep breath. 'It's about me and Ken: we ain't married. I never said we was, mind – you just thought it. But I never put you right, so that's just as bad. I don't know why I done it – it just seemed easier like.'

'So he's not in Northern Ireland.'

She shook her head. 'No. At least, I don't think so.'

'He's left you, has he?'

'Yes.' The admission was easier to make than she expected. She felt no desperate pang. In fact, it came as a relief.

'And do you miss him?'

'No. Well, yes, sometimes. But I don't want him back. Never.' Was it true? She thought it was.

'Well, then,' he said, smiling a broad smile. 'That's all right then, isn't it?'

He reached out to touch her hand, and she spilled her tea. 'Oh, Christ,' she said and jumped up to get a cloth from the kitchen, regretting her choice of swearword. Clyde would think even less of her now.

'Sorry,' she said when she had cleared up the mess. 'I don't know why I done that. Nerves, I suppose.'

'That's all right,' he said, taking her hand successfully this time. 'I'm not going to eat you up. Look at me.'

She turned her face towards him, and he snarled like a tiger.

They both laughed.

'You're not angry with me, then?' she asked.

'Not at all,' he said. 'It's the best news I've had in a long time.'

He leant forward, and she let him kiss her.

At last the grey landscape comes to an end. The wind slackens and deposits Kit on the edge of a valley. As he looks down into it, he blinks. Colours – wild, extravagant colours – assault his eyes, which struggle with them as they would with light after hours in a darkened room. They are colours of the jungle: bold red and sharp emerald, languid yellow and glaring blue, their vividness carrying Kit back momentarily to the aquarium at Kew Gardens. But this is only a half-thought, a glimpse of a world which seems itself to be confined behind glass, existing in another element.

Above all, there is green: sheaves of fat green leaves splayed out in lavish bushes; clusters of them borne towards the sky, crowning slender, arched trees; vines abseiling from lost heights towards a thick, yielding carpet of vegetation. The thin, sterile dust has no place here. Yet there is something which disturbs Kit about this valley – something more unsettling than mere surprise.

After a few minutes he begins to discern human figures in the jungle terrain. Whether they have gradually emerged from hiding or were in front of his eyes all along, he cannot say; but certainly their lack of vigour, indeed of perceptible motion, makes it unlikely that they have come from – or are going – anywhere. They lie in the deep grass or stretched along branches of trees or slumped against trunks, moored but not imprisoned by the creepers around them.

Kit feels emboldened to approach. Here he senses he is no longer an intruder: he is as legitimate a part of the scene as the parakeets whose wings ruffle the silence or the startling orchids sprinkled on the banks below, their petals spread wide and stamens thrust forward like small radio-telescopes. He makes his way down the bank.

The first figure he comes to is lying on his side. He is a strong, healthy-looking man with long dark hair and a thick beard. His eyes are wide open yet his breathing is shallow, as if he were asleep. He appears not to notice the newcomer. Kit greets him.

It has no effect. Kit kneels beside him and speaks again, more loudly. The man stirs a little but still seems unaware of his presence. Kit shakes him by the shoulder, and he comes to consciousness.

As he does, the entire landscape changes. The parakeets soaring through air disappear into blue nothingness as if they had never been. The orchids spread their petals with visible speed, then are gone too, bright colours fading against leaves like fireworks that burst and vanish in a night sky. The leaves themselves become insubstantial, transparent as mere projections upon a screen vying with daylight, until all that remains in view are bleached trunks and branches, jutting out of naked terrain. It is like watching a dog shaking water from its coat, this banishing of colour, or a demonstration of centrifugal force.

In an instant, it all changes again. Colours ripple back, as vivid as ever – the deep greens of leaves and prodigal splashes of flowers. Kit thinks of an old toy his mother gave him, a scratched plastic bubble filled with water, containing a tiny cottage around which snow appeared to whirl when you rolled it over before finally settling. This moment was like the settling of the snow, and there was something wonderful yet disappointing about its calmness. He looks down at the man on the ground beside him and sees that he has relapsed into unconsciousness.

He recognises now that this landscape is something dreamed by the man and his companions. He understands why he himself does not appear to be an intruder, for anything real or unreal can be drawn into their world of imagination and have equal validity in it.

Just to be sure, he makes his way further down the valley and attempts to rouse a woman sleeping with her back against the base of a tree. The effect is the same: the colours and vegetation ebb away, then shiver back again as her head drops in new slumber. But as Kit considers his next move, he hears a voice calling to him.

'You are wasting your time. They are drunk with dreams, and there is no waking them. Best leave them alone.'

The voice appears to be coming from his right. Looking round, he notices a half-overgrown path leading down into a clearing. He follows it and finds himself standing beside a broad river, which moves at such speed that anyone entering the water would instantly be swept away. There is, however, a safe way of crossing it: a wooden bridge with a gate at the near end, reached by a small set of steps.

The land on the far side is more orderly than the jungle through which Kit has come. It is no less green or colourful, but the trees do not attempt to block out the light – the first sunlight he has seen since his arrival in this world, its bright beams skating through deferential leaves. The undergrowth does not impede his steps, and the flowers – though still profuse – are no longer overwhelming. Neither threatening nor tame, the scene seems exciting and familiar.

He sees the person who must have called to him. A man is standing by the gate on the bridge with his back to Kit, tending a profusion of roses, which grow in a tall arch. As Kit approaches, the man turns around, showing the skin of his face and hands to be wrinkled like an old apple's; but there is a boyishness about his smile that suggests a spirit much younger than his body. Here too Kit feels a sense of familiarity, yet he is quite sure that he has never seen this man before.

'Hold these, will you?' says the stranger with a smile, handing Kit a pair of secateurs. 'I'll be with you in just a moment.' He turns back to his work, lifting a blossom that has fallen away, interweaving its stem with another so as to hold it securely in place. 'No greenfly here, of course,' he remarks as he takes a step back to scrutinise his handiwork. 'That's the greatest blessing. Yes, I think that will do. How does it look to you?'

'Very beautiful,' says Kit.

'It does, doesn't it? Very beautiful. Good. Well, I'll take those secateurs off you.' Kit hands them back.

'Thank you,' says the old man, putting them in the pocket of an apron he wears. 'Now, have you managed to work out who I am?'

The smile becomes even wider. 'I'm your mother's grandfather,' he says. 'Welcome, Kit. Welcome home.'

10.

My charter flight reached Izmir in the early hours. A bus was waiting outside to take us to Bodrum. Once aboard I dozed as best I could, trying to ignore the grunts of a drunken couple stretched out on the back seat.

In wakeful moments I wondered what kind of reception I would get from my mother. It was more than two years since I'd seen her; at that meeting she had spoken so venomously of Dad that it had been a relief to say goodbye. Would she be horrified? Would she berate me for failing to warn of my arrival? Or would she fling her arms around me and tell me that she'd been a failure as a mother but would find a way of making it up?

The cheapest way of getting to Turkey had been to buy a package holiday. Mine included accommodation at the Pension Diana, a half-completed building on a steep hill not far from the town centre. My room was more comfortable than I expected, with a shower and proper British-style loo. An enormous poster of fjords occupied most of one wall. The sheets were slightly damp, but I was so tired that I scarcely noticed. I climbed between them and slept until midday.

On waking I wandered down to the harbour in search of lunch. The Pension Diana, it was clear, was not the only place racing to extend its facilities before the next deluge of tourists: the town reverberated with cement mixers; everywhere teams of workmen were throwing together walls and roofs with, it seemed, more haste than attention to detail. The dust raised drifted on a light breeze and mingled with that from white, un-tarmacked roads before settling on everything in sight. Even the cross-bred dogs which wandered the streets looked faintly bleached.

The waterfront, overlooked by a Crusader castle, was a wonderful sight. Rows of highly varnished yachts gleamed in the sunshine. I shot off a couple of rolls of film before sitting down outside a small restaurant to order stuffed vine leaves and red mullet. Having eaten, I finally felt equal to the task of tracking down my mother.

After the failure of my attempts to telephone, I didn't attach much hope to her last known address; but I got directions from a waiter and headed off into the little streets, past a school playground where a rudimentary band made up of tiny children was parading up and down. Eventually I found myself outside a whitewashed house much like every other house in the town, its block-like façade enlivened by a chimney stack and an arched entrance to a courtyard.

Here I found a grey-haired, moustachioed man wrapped in a large coat – although the day was sunny, it was far from warm. He was reading a newspaper generously illustrated with off-register colour photographs. This I guessed to be the person with whom I had spoken on the phone; if it was, his English had not improved in the intervening weeks. I tried French and German, but he merely shook his head. As a last resort, I rummaged in my wallet and produced a photo of Mum.

His face lit up. He nodded vigorously, tapped me on the shoulder to indicate that I should remain where I was and disappeared inside, returning with a pencil and scrap of paper on which he drew a crude map. I recognised the harbour and castle and what appeared to be a mosque; somewhere between them was a cross which I took to represent my missing parent.

Only when I got back to the waterfront did the inadequacy of the map become apparent. The cross lay in an area traversed by a score of streets, all of which contained a generous number of tourist shops. There was nothing for it but to take out Mum's photo again and show it to anyone who seemed a fixture in the area.

As it turned out, I was first time lucky. Stepping into a corner shop whose doorway was hung with burnished copper pans and ornaments, I endeavoured to explain myself to a large, smiling man in a grey leather jacket. Yes, he spoke English; yes, he would be happy to look at the photo. He took it in his pudgy hand and, after moving towards the window for more light, emitted a roar of laughter.

'Susan!' he exclaimed.

'So you know her?'

'Yes, yes. Everyone in Bodrum knows Susan.'

I didn't quite know how to take this. Had my mother become a character – the sort of expatriate who cultivates eccentricities and gets drunk every night? Or was it merely the warmth of her personality which had endeared her to the locals?

'Are you her son?'

I nodded, and another healthy laugh shook his impressive frame.

Then he shouted something in Turkish, and a woman emerged from the back of the shop. She seemed to find the photograph as funny as he did and stared at me in hilarious wonder.

'Come,' said the man, putting an arm round my shoulders. 'Your mother's shop is very near. I will show you.'

He steered me along the street, occasionally shouting to other shopkeepers and pointing to me with an enormous grin. They grinned back. I began to feel like an early aviator flying into a hick town which had never seen an aeroplane before. Although this was embarrassing, I was afterwards grateful, because it prepared me for a rare experience – seeing my mother through new eyes.

We found her sitting on a bench in the sun, drinking silty Turkish coffee with three men – two of them definitely European, the third local, though with his elegant clothes he could have passed for Italian. Mum was telling some story which they seemed to find funny, because they rocked with laughter as she contorted her arms in increasingly wild gestures. She was wearing a long, boldly patterned skirt and white cotton jersey and had bangles glistening on her wrist.

I couldn't believe how beautiful she looked. At our last meeting in London her face had been strained and grey, her mouth tight and drawing desperately on a succession of cigarettes. It was as if twenty years had been torn from her like a latex mask, and the neurotic divorcee had reverted to a carefree young woman. As I watched her being admired by those men, who clearly believed no company could be more glamorous than this radiant ex-model's, I thought how lucky I was to be her son.

'Susan!' cried my guide. 'A visitor!'

She looked up at me, squinting into the sun, and I thought for a terrible moment that the spell was about to be broken: that the white-washed walls around us might collapse into nettle-infested ruins, the laughing men be snatched into invisibility and my mother left ranting at me, a deformed crone in black rags. Instead, as her eyes grew wide again in recognition, she sprang to her feet and ran forward to hug me.

'Darling!'

She had never called me 'darling' in her life, yet there was nothing false about it: it was like a throwback to my grandparents' world, the kind of expression that would have filled her teenage conversation if she hadn't hung out with my father and Robbie and people who said 'baby' the whole time.

'Hi Mum.' We held each other, and though half embarrassed by the onlookers, I basked in the moment. I hadn't expected it and hadn't expected to be so glad of it.

'What in the world are you doing here?' she asked. Suddenly she looked anxious. 'Has something happened? Is Granny all right?'

'Nothing's happened. I've just come to see you, that's all.'

'Thank goodness for that.' She gave a little laugh. 'Well, now, let me introduce you to everyone. This is Suleiman' – she indicated the dapper Turk – 'and Simon, and Toby. And this, everybody,' she added, making me feel thirteen again, 'is my enormous son.'

I shook hands and thanked the shopkeeper who had escorted me. He grinned and withdrew, a master of ceremonies whose duties had been fulfilled.

The others made to excuse themselves, but Mum insisted they finish their coffee. An awkward ten minutes ensued during which they politely questioned me about my flight, what I got up to in London and so on.

When they had gone, Mum showed me round her shop: a modest place, stocked mainly with swim-suits, T-shirts, sunhats and inexpensive jewellery. Then she locked up, and we drove off to collect my bag from the Pension Diana, negotiating monstrous potholes on the way.

'Tourists always come here expecting the roads to be terrible,' she remarked, 'but actually out in the countryside they're not bad at all. It's the streets around town that murder your suspension.'

Her house – a small but comfortable bungalow – lay on a grassy hillside a few miles away. Crumbled stone walls in the fields suggested that there had once been a small community here, but Mum's only immediate neighbours were a handful of goats. The sea could just be glimpsed in the distance.

Not until I'd unpacked and slept a bit more, and was sitting on the terrace with a drink in my hand as darkness started to fall, did I find the strength to explain the reason for my visit. Mum put down her glass and suddenly looked her anxious London self again.

'I'm sorry, darling,' she said. 'I'm afraid you're too late.'

Life was brighter now for Stella. Her flat, though no more comfortable, was suddenly less oppressive. Since Clyde had shown her how to laugh at its shortcomings, she had begun to think of it as a sort of three-dimensional practical joke whose every crack and damp patch had been devised by unseen powers to try her patience. To shout and weep about it was to give in to her tormentors: better by far to go along with the gag, refusing to be wound up.

The houses where she worked, too, took on a new attraction. She started to enjoy the contents more, not allowing herself to become diverted from work or coveting the things around her, but seeing them as something to aspire to. While she knew that she was unlikely ever to own a house as big as the Elliots' or a sofa quite as opulent as the Weiners', the world through which she moved with her duster seemed less alien. Like a new recruit to a crack regiment, hoping to work her way up through the ranks, she polished the Coopers' brass-framed table as assiduously as a button on a general's tunic and wielded her Hoover with as much care as a mine-detector.

Only during the brief coffee breaks which she allowed herself, ten minutes in the middle of a three-hour session, did she let her curiosity get the better of her. Drinking coffee, she decided, was not the best way to spend these periods: instead, she browsed bookshelves, examined silverware and passed her fingers over the clothes that hung primly in her employers' wardrobes. Mrs Elliot had a particularly magnificent array of suits and dresses, wool and silk and cotton in all the colours of the rainbow, spotlessly clean, smartly cut, hanging rail upon rail in strip-lit cupboards flanked by full-length mirrors, dozens of pairs of shoes paraded in racks below them. Mrs Elliot herself was always as immaculately turned out as a model. She was the most exacting of the women Stella worked for.

The awe which she inspired made the wardrobe supremely tempting. It occurred to Stella that if she was to try on one of the bold suits with gilt buttons, the distance between them might shrink and some of her employer's self-possession rub off on her. But she never did so, partly through fear of being caught in the act and partly because it would be the crossing of an invisible line, a violation of trust.

The place she liked best was Sebastian Terry's. She always looked forward to the ten minutes a week when she could sit down and turn the pages of one of his albums, taken from the pile beneath the coffee-table in his living-room. Since she now knew him to be a professional photographer, this seemed more permissible, though she was never absolutely sure that she might not stumble on forbidden territory.

Above all, she was taken by a portfolio of what appeared at first to be abstracts: strange, grainy forms which loomed out from stiff pages like dreams squeezed onto paper and trapped in shiny flatness, yet still straining to escape definition and drift away down tunnels of metamorphosis. As she stared at them, she could half believe that they

103

were changing shape in front of her eyes. If only, she thought, she might enter a world where self and surroundings could be altered at will, as if you were wandering from set to set in a gigantic film studio and could step into any role you fancied and play it for as long as you liked. She had always imagined that heaven was like that: not a place with angels sitting on clouds playing harps, but exactly what every individual wanted it to be – a nice pub or dance-floor or country lane. But there was no point in filling your head with idle thoughts; you might as well spend your life taking crack or Ecstasy or whatever it was the kids on the estate were into. There were shelves to dust and floors to mop if she was going to get anywhere, and here she was, gawping at photographs of mushrooms.

She felt more optimistic about Kit now. He was still terribly, terribly quiet, but the vacancy which had filled his eyes seemed by imperceptible degrees to have vanished; and though he might not respond to her, she could have sworn that he was aware of her presence. It was wonderful, she thought, the way things could heal without doctors or medicines. Maybe the music she had been playing him really was doing the trick.

As for herself, when they were standing waiting for the bus and she was thinking about Clyde, it was an old Aretha Franklin song that she found going round in her head. 'You make me feel,' she hummed, 'like a natural woman.'

Kit gazes at his great-grandfather and thinks that he has never seen a person so good and kind and wise and contented. All these qualities are in the old man's face, giving it – despite wrinkles and crevices – a radiant clarity. Instinctively, he embraces him. As a large, rough hand clasps the back of his head, he feels the anxiety of grey limbo draining from him. When the last of it has gone, he looks up at the old man and asks, 'Where am I?'

The old man smiles broadly, and laughs. 'Don't you recognise it?'

Kit gazes around. 'I know the sky,' he says, 'and the trees and fields, and the birdsong and fox coverts, and the secret pathways through the woods, and the steep banks and shadows that move with the breeze. But not this bridge, and not this river.'

'These are the borders of heaven,' says his great-grandfather. 'Few of its inhabitants walk this way. It is a place of arrival, not departure. This is the Bridge of Relief.'

Kit looks more closely at the structure and sees that the wood from which it is made – slats, handrails, trellis-work – is of an unfamiliar kind, strong, dark and richly polished. Crouching, he runs his fingers over it and asks his great-grandfather what it is.

'It is like nothing you know, for it is made of many things together: the touch of a farmer's hand, patting his horse's neck as he stands on a cold morning and surveys the pastures where a flood has receded; the sound of wheels on a runway as an aeroplane comes in to land; the dust on two travellers' feet as they find the path which will lead them down to the valley; the narrowing of a thirsty labourer's eyes as he takes a draught from his glass of beer; the first rays of morning light above a sick man's rumpled bed; the grip of an earthquake-survivor's hands as he hauls himself from the rubble; the sound of applause on the opening night of a play; the relaxing of the impala's ears as the lion's roar dies; the clenching of a defendant's hands as the jury declares him not guilty; the disbelief on a sentinel's face as he glimpses a faraway banner moving towards his besieged city; a housewife's silent prayer as her hand closes on a lost key; the hiss of a final flame doused by a fireman's hose; a schoolboy's gaze as he learns from a notice-board that he has passed his final exams; the sinking of tired limbs into a hot bath; the waking of drought-stricken villagers to the sound of heavy rain; the trembling of a lover who finds the courage to declare himself.

'All these things grow together in a single tree; and that tree grows in a forest where many fugitives have found shelter, fugitives from cruelty and injustice and despair; and this bridge is made from the wood of that tree.'

Kit leans against the side of the bridge and begins to cry. His great-grandfather kneels down beside him and holds him in his arms as he weeps for the world's sadness – the bleakness of the estate, his mother's loneliness, the harsh voices of people railing against their lot, the long, desperate search for an undefined something else. His tears explode against the slats of the bridge and seep through to join the waters that flow beneath it.

'Come with me,' says the old man at last, when the sobbing has died. He helps Kit to his feet and leads him to the other parapet, where he points far upstream. 'Look over there.'

Kit follows the line of his arm and sees that the river below them emerges from a delta where seven other rivers have come together. They could, he thinks, be described as lesser rivers; yet each is so mighty in its own right that the word is inappropriate. They seem at once to flow down from the sky and break from beneath the earth, rushing vigorously, glinting in the sun.

The fertile plains through which they run appear to applaud their progress. Now the ears of corn are a million upraised hands; now they are a heavy golden mane. The rivers are a seven-branched candlestick, burnished till the gold from which it is fashioned infuses the air with its gleam.

'These are the rivers,' says Kit's great-grandfather, 'that flow between heaven and earth, and between earth and heaven.'

'Where do they begin?' Kit asks.

'They begin at the fountain of life, and they end in the ocean of eternity; but the fountain is never exhausted, and the ocean is never full. And when they reach that delta, they mingle with each other and with springs you cannot see to form the river of life, encompassing everything men know and imagine and what they have yet to imagine. In its waters are mingled past and present and future, actuality and possibility.'

'They're beautiful,' says Kit. 'I had forgotten how beautiful things could be. I have been looking too long at mirages.'

'Not at mirages but in mirrors, obscured by drifts of spray. Here you can see to the heart of the waters. Look at the river on the extreme left and tell me what you find.'

Kit focuses on the river indicated, the first flank of the candelabra. 'I see a chemist in a laboratory,' he says, 'surrounded by flasks and clamps and test tubes and tripods, grasping a piece of paper as if it had been given to him in a dream. I see an actress on a podium grasping a trophy, and a child admiring the great height of a castle he has built on the sands of a broad bay.'

His great-grandfather nods his head. 'The first of the rivers is the river of triumph. What about the river beside it?'

Kit screws up his eyes and looks again. 'An old woman who smiles and lays aside a piece of lace she has made; a host who watches his friends laughing as they eat and drink at his table, drawn closer by his generosity; a herdsman scanning a green pasture and counting out the full number of his cattle; a kestrel that sees its young wheeling through the sky; a couple walking through their new house when the last piece of furniture has been set in place.'

'The second of the rivers is the river of satisfaction. Now look into the river on its right and tell me what you see there.'

'I see a man in the corner of a railway carriage, chuckling to himself over a book, and a girl in a cinema with a broad smile on her face; two schoolboys convulsed over a joke, and a happy crowd gathered around a clown in a city square; a young woman watching the man she loves as he flails on an ice-rink with uncertain feet.'

'And what river do you think that is?'

'The river of laughter?'

The old man nods. 'Again,' he says.

Kit focuses on the central river. 'A man stares at a baby as he cradles it in his hands, wondering at its fragility. A boy and a dog splash through a muddy lane, the dog barking and dancing round in circles, the boy kicking a football for him to chase. A man and a woman walk laughing along a wet pavement as heavy raindrops splash against their faces. Two friends, happening upon each other after many years apart, embrace with tears and delight. A girl fingers a letter she has read so often that the paper has worn thin. This must be the river of loving.'

His great-grandfather shakes his head. 'No, not just that: it is the river of loving and being loved, for here there is no distinction between them. Try the next.'

'I see an architect poring over plans of a house; a child colouring a picture with many different crayons, her lips pursed, deaf to all around her; a gardener easing a plant from its pot into the soil; an old tailor with calloused hands unfurling a bolt of dark, soft cloth; a photographer assembling the elements of a still life; a typographer hesitating between fonts.'

'That is the river of creativity. And now, the penultimate branch of the delta.'

'In this one... a nurse pausing to reassure a patient's anxious relative; a voluntary worker in a choking slum tending a malnourished child; a woman in the prime of life caring for a wheelchair-bound patient; a missionary helping to educate an isolated tribe, far from the streets where he played as a child and the family which loves him.'

'That river,' says the old man, 'is the river of selflessness.'

Kit is puzzled. 'But...' he objects.

'Yes?'

'In limbo I saw many people who had abandoned their dreams to live through others. What is the difference between them and these?'

'It is simple enough. Living *for* others is not the same as living *through* others: for many it is their dream, not the negation of it. There is no greater fulfilment than in helping your fellow men; what matters is not to use others as an excuse for abandoning your own allotted goal. But the final river – tell me what you see there.'

Kit looks for the last time and sees a river which seems to shine more brightly than the others, to flow more powerfully and send the sound of its waters more musically on the air. 'A nun,' he says, 'so deep in prayer that the anxieties of the world and all that she has done and been and all that she has desired and enjoyed and all that she has known of happiness and unhappiness are forgotten. A writer sitting at his desk, having reached such a pitch of thought that the words come more quickly than his pen can write. And a couple after long separation, misunderstanding and doubt, consummating their love.'

'You have sharp eyes,' says his great-grandfather. 'They have shown you the river of ecstasy, and if you turn them to the great torrent below this bridge you will understand the river of life. Gaze first on the waters which flow nearest the sky, then look through them to the waters which flow beneath and see what men on earth can only dream of.'

So Kit leans over the parapet and watches the river surge past them as if flowing through space, unconfined, knowing no friction, shaped only by its will. He focuses on the surface and first gradation of light below it and sees the sun rise as if through an open window. So vivid is the picture that he can feel the coolness of air and depth of wet grass and hear the stirrings of waking cattle and brave song of the skylark as it climbs. He sees the flowers unfurling heavy petals and a hare trying its limbs in the first foray of morning, bolting across an empty meadow like a child late for school. Now as the sun grows brighter with every moment, throwing its light across the world like a bird spreading its wings, a man steps out onto a country road that runs away before him, dropping into a valley, then rising in a shallow curve to lose itself among distant hills. Where it goes, the man does not know; all that matters is that it is open before him. So he settles his pack on his back, pauses a minute to watch the joyful whirling of the lark and, taking a stick from the hedgerow in his hand and whistling in imitation of a tiny bird's song, strides off towards whatever the day may hold.

Kit looks again, this time into darker and deeper waters, and sees a man and a woman sitting at a broad oak table in front of a small farmhouse, their day's work done. The sun is setting and the woods around them appear to be slipping into sleep as shadows step forward like attentive footmen, ready to clear away the day. A breeze from a nearby lake rearranges the hair on the woman's forehead. Away in the distance, lights from a town are beginning to shine out, echoing the first stars. Unseen and barely heard, an otter slips into the lake. The woman laughs; the man smiles. They reach for each other's hands.

'Euphoria and contentment,' says Kit's great-grandfather. 'On earth you can hope at best for one or the other; here, as you see, they flow together – morning and evening, energy and rest, the beginning and end. Now see where the river goes.'

And he turns and leads Kit to the other parapet.

'What do you mean, too late?' I asked. I could feel my heart skittering like a football, bounce-bounce-bouncing down a flight of steps.

My mother pulled on her cigarette. 'Your father sent me the papers by courier two weeks ago. He said that the sitting tenant at the cottage, Mr whatever his name was – '

'Czernowsky.'

' – had died and that he was hoping for a quick sale and thought it would help if he and I got our side of things sorted out straight away. He enclosed estimates from three estate agents and offered me half of the highest one, cash down, before he'd even sold the place. I must admit it seemed a little odd of him to behave quite so generously, but I thought maybe this unfortunate woman he'd dragged to the registry office had had some miraculous effect on him. Anyway, with my overdraft in the state it was, I couldn't afford to say no. Now I can buy a lot of new stock and stop worrying about whether I'm going to make it through another year here.'

'And have you had the money?'

She nodded. 'It was paid into my account ten days ago. That reptilian bank manager is my new best friend.'

'And there was Dad telling me how hard up he was,' I said bitterly. 'If he can lay his hands on that kind of money overnight, he can't be doing that badly.'

I looked towards the town and imagined lights from boats glimmering cheerfully along the waterfront. It was difficult to take in what Mum had said, to accept that my father had outmanoeuvred me as ruthlessly as if I had been the head of a rival advertising agency. But after all, my own reasons for coming here had not been any different. It was just that he'd been quicker and smarter.

'Didn't you know that he'd promised the cottage to me?' I asked reproachfully.

'No,' she said. 'How could I? You've never discussed it with me. He certainly didn't tell me.'

'I'm sorry,' I said, after a moment's silence, reaching out and squeezing her hand. 'That wasn't fair. It's simply that I had my heart set on living there. I suppose it's the place that I think of as home.'

Mum smiled. 'We had some good times there, didn't we?'

'I ought to tell you,' I said, 'that you were wrong about Vicky. If anyone did the dragging to the registry office it was her. They're both up to their necks in this.'

'Thank God for Turkey,' said Mum. 'I don't have to see them, or even think about them much. But I wish you hadn't been pulled into it. I suppose your father feels that in some tortuous way he's getting at me through you.

'I wish there was something I could do, darling,' she continued. 'But I can hardly ring him up and say I've changed my mind about selling the cottage – he wouldn't give me the time of day. And my new friend the bank manager would kill me.'

We sat in silence for a bit. It really was silent: no wind, no traffic, no human beings, until eventually a couple of wayfarers passed invisibly on the other side of the house, deep in conversation, and headed on down the hill – hungry for supper, I imagined, after a hard day.

'It's partly my fault,' I said at last. 'If I'd been better at keeping in touch with you this might never have happened.'

'I haven't exactly been the world's greatest letter-writer either,' she said. 'But life's too short to worry about what might have been. It's very nice to have you here now.' She got up and ruffled my hair the way she used to when I was a child. 'What about some supper?'

'Can I give you a hand?' I asked.

'Don't worry. It's nothing very elaborate. A few local specialities.'

I remained on the terrace, sipping my glass of Turkish wine. It was easy to see the attraction of the place. I didn't feel abandoned by Mum; in fact, I was glad that her continuing good looks hadn't made her the third wife of a fat old businessman in Surrey – though at the same time rather relieved that she wasn't living here with a medallioned toy boy.

Over supper we talked about Robbie.

'I'm glad he's got someone to look after him,' she said. 'She sounds nice, this Sabrina. But I do wonder what will become of him.'

'Apparently there's some rich Texan who's very interested in his work,' I said. 'Robbie thinks it could be his big break.'

She gave a sad little smile. 'There's always a rich Texan. And he always loses interest at the last moment. I'm afraid that's the story of your uncle's life.'

It was a shock to hear her say such a thing. I suppose that in my heart of hearts I had long assumed my uncle was destined for a life of failure; but that wasn't the same as being told by someone else – someone who loved him as much as I did.

'You never know,' I said weakly.

'No,' she said, not pressing the point.

At last I plucked up the courage to ask her. 'Mum, why did Dad and Robbie fall out?'

For a moment I thought she was going to pretend she hadn't heard the question. Then she sighed and looked at me: 'I promised myself, mainly for your sake, that I would never tell anyone. But it seems to me that your father has forfeited whatever loyalty you and I once had to him, and I think it's probably best that you know.

'Your father and Robbie were the closest friends you can imagine. They lived together, painted together, partied together. In fact, for a period of about two years they were so inseparable that I literally can't remember seeing one without the other. The one worrying thing was the difference in their talent. Robbie really was very accomplished, whereas your father was promising but no more. Robbie wasn't competitive, but to your father it mattered a lot: I think he saw his painting as his way of getting on in life, and when Robbie got a first and he didn't, he took it badly. I don't think their friendship was ever quite the same after that. Being totally infatuated with your father at that stage, I agonised about how it would all end – whether he would spend the rest of his life in the shadow of my brother.

'As it turned out, neither of them had any immediate success after college, so they decided to visit America and see what kind of reception their work got there. In those days it was a big deal going to New York – you didn't just flit over for the weekend the way people do now – and they were both incredibly excited about it: the New World, rock and roll, pop culture. For weeks beforehand they spent the whole time talking in American accents and acting out scenes from Westerns.

'When they got there, things went pretty well. Several galleries expressed interest in seeing more of their work; the hip types in Greenwich Village liked having these two good-looking English boys around, and staid types on Fifth Avenue were impressed by your grandfather's title, so in one way or other they did the whole scene. One of the people they got to meet was Andy Warhol, who invited them to go round and visit him the following day.

'What exactly happened next only your father knows. I don't think there's much doubt that they were both doing a lot of drugs, and Robbie being Robbie was doing more than your father. The one definite fact is that when it was time to visit Andy Warhol, your uncle wasn't in a fit state to go. When he surfaced the day after, your father told him that he'd taken both their portfolios to Warhol, who was so excited that he wanted them to go back to London and paint enough pictures for a big joint exhibition in six months' time, which he would personally organise. There was not a moment to lose, and Tony rushed Robbie home to England.

'Well, the exhibition never came off. According to your father, Warhol became obsessed with film-making at that point and couldn't spare the time or money. Robbie seemed to take it harder than he did: he kept saying that it was his fault for missing the meeting, and Warhol probably didn't trust him to produce the goods.

'Your father was much more stoical about it. He pointed out that they'd had plenty of interest from other people and that their best move would be to go back with another lot of paintings. Unfortunately, they were very low on cash, so it was decided that only one of them should make the trip; and since your father was generally more reliable and a better salesman, he got the ticket.

'Not long after he arrived, he sent Robbie a letter with a money order to reimburse him for the half of the ticket he'd paid for. The letter said that he'd got sucked into Warhol's film project, and it seemed too good an opportunity to miss; he wasn't going to have time to haul their portfolios around the galleries, but he hoped that Robbie would under- stand and forgive him – which Robbie being Robbie did, saying that as soon as he got some more money he'd head out there himself. But it never happened.

'After that, it was your father who had everything going his way. He worked with Warhol on a couple more films and then came back and made *Innuendo*. The rest, as they say, is history.

'It wasn't until years later that Robbie found out what really hap- pened at the meeting he missed with Andy Warhol. He ran into an American at the Arts Club who had actually been there. This man, whose name was De Fries, said the occasion had stuck in his mind because Warhol had been so impressed by your father's portfolio: De Fries didn't think it more than good of its kind, but there was some- thing in it which really seemed to touch a nerve with Andy. According to De Fries, Warhol hadn't suggested an exhibition at all: he had invited your father then and there to take part in his film project.

'It was obvious to Robbie that De Fries's memory wasn't as good as he thought it was: after all, why should your father want to lie about something like that? But then De Fries started describing one of the paintings that had made this big impression on Warhol. And the thing was it wasn't one of your father's at all – it was one of Robbie's.

'So that was it – the reason why your father had been so keen to get Robbie back to London. He had deliberately passed off Robbie's work as his own and needed to have him out of the way in case he got chatting to Warhol and they discovered the truth.

'Of course, there's no telling how things might have turned out if Robbie had been at the meeting. It could be that your father was the inferior painter but the better film-maker and that he made the most of a chance that Robbie would have blown. But it could equally well be that he robbed him of his opportunity to become one of the biggest artists of the decade – and who knows what that disappointment contributed to Robbie becoming an addict.'

'What did Robbie do when he found out?'

'Nothing, as far as I know. You know what he's like – the least vindictive person in the world. He wasn't seeing much of your father by that stage, and he told me there was no point in getting upset over something that had happened so long ago. In fact, I think, I was a good deal angrier about it than he was. I tried to have it out with your father, but he simply denied the whole thing.'

'How could Dad do that,' I said. 'Betray his best friend?'

My mother reached out and took my hand. 'He hasn't treated you any better, has he, darling? Or me, for that matter. Perhaps only someone with a gift for making dreams can be so adept at destroying them.'

11.

'Listen,' says the old man.

At first Kit hears only the rushing of water; but then, as when a kettle on the hob moves from silence to singing, he becomes aware of sound building towards music, ripples becoming notes, until – all gathered in one vast orchestration – they seem to fill the air, running through his hair, washing his cheeks and brow, engulfing his ears, drenching him with harmony. The music that his mother has played him on the radio, the high raptures of the greatest symphonies, are like snatches of a minor variation in terms of this great whole. Some of the sounds are familiar, but among the known instruments are others never heard or long forgotten, and beside human voices are voices of other creatures that he does not recognise, haunting and sweet, as if his heart were a harp on which they played, or as if the river were engulfing him. He feels himself flowing with it as he watches, borne through caves and down mountainsides, dashing among chasms where a thousand interwoven melodies re-echo from rocky walls.

'Let me drown!' he exclaims, head thrown back and mouth open wide to catch the cool spray. 'Let me drown in music.'

'Watch.'

So Kit watches and sees the river which is music move as if to music, like a serpent delighting in its motion, or a vortex spinning for pure light-heartedness. As he watches, the sky changes from daylight to twilight, and the river rises to flow across it in a bold arch. Stars uncountable, incomprehensible, spread out against a rich and gentle darkness like treasures garnered by a fearless merchant beyond the known boundaries of the world and thrown out on lengths of soft and precious fabric to astound his monarch's eye. But the stars are not stars as seen from the earth: their positions are not fixed but move with the flow and music of the river. They do not move violently like shooting stars, but neatly and regularly, weaving in and out of each other like well-rehearsed dancers. Kit stares, mesmerised by their motion. Their energy dizzies him; his mind fumbles with the way in which layer folds into layer and rank breaks and recombines with rank. Even he who has played among the planets knows nothing as beautiful as this ribbon of infinity, scintillating, undulating like a flock of silver starlings seeking their nests at nightfall. As the stars whirl and climb and drift and retire, they seem still to grow in number, with new glints like half-formed thoughts stealing through the darkness and mushrooming into constellations of pure light.

Then he notices an impediment in the river: a dark shape, like a boulder, breaking its flow and creating a discordant eddy. Puzzled, he turns to his companion. 'What is it?' he asks. 'Surely it cannot belong here? Why is it not removed?'

'It will be,' says his great-grandfather. 'But for now, let it remind you that the beauty of the river is not to be taken for granted. If you are brave, look more closely at it; but do not expect to enjoy what you see.'

Kit stares more intently at the rock, and as he does, its surface appears to become shinier – not shining like silver, but with an intense blackness – until it has the reflective quality of a mirror. But what he sees in it is not himself or the celestial panorama around, but a road which is in neither the countryside nor the city but a place half of brick and half of earth. It is a place of restriction and confinement, where possibilities are diminished and frustration feeds on itself; where nightfall does not bring true darkness and no birds herald dawn; where sunlight pushes through thin curtains, and windows stare at walls. A wheelbarrow rusts in a garden; fat paperback novels curl on shelves. The houses smell of stale air and decay.

Kit sees a young boy running after a group of older children, begging to be included in their games. They stop and call him to them, putting him through a catechism of obscenities, laughing at his eagerness to learn things whose meaning and effect he cannot understand.

Kit sees a man with his wrist in plaster crying out for help, and the flash of faces at the windows, and unopened doors.

He sees a gardener in a park nurturing bedding plants, and heavy boots coming to trample them down.

He sees a boxing promoter smiling as the crowd shouts for blood.

He sees a thief stealing a wedding ring.

He sees a religious fanatic planting a bomb in a bus station.

He sees a man who feigns need soliciting the charity of others.

'In all those instances,' says the old man, 'people have cut themselves off from the river and entered what some call hell. The last you saw is the worst, for his is a double sin: a crime which depends on the goodness of its victims. Many embrace the way of negation: the failure to acknowledge what brings us together, to empathise with our fellows. But to wrong a man who shows you right – that is the fastest way to work your own destruction.'

'The rock is changing,' says Kit.

'It is.'

The rock appears to grow smoother and smaller, worn away by the passing stars. As it does so the music of the river grows still louder and more beautiful. 'One day,' says the old man, 'it will vanish completely. But until then, think of this stone as a whetstone, sharpening man's taste for goodness.'

So Kit turns his eyes away from the rock and becomes aware of the shape the river describes in the heavens. He sees that it is a great spiral, moving outwards from a point invisible to him to a circle encompassing more than he can see. Again the light changes: the sky pales, and an incipient pink – like that of dawn when night still hesitates above field and forest – washes across the surface of the river, colouring it like polished recesses of a shell.

Then it seems to Kit that a shell is what the river has become, its spirals tracing a smooth, strong form more beautiful than the carapaces of dwellers in deepest oceans or those that feel their watery way across coral reefs in the warm Antipodes; durable as adamant, robust as any bulwark, yet more delicate in its multifarious hues than the richest mother-of-pearl or most extravagant orchid, with colours and iridescence that sing like the voices of the river, bringing tears to Kit's eyes. The shell serves two purposes: on the one hand it gathers in all the sounds that are in the universe – of winds and waves, men and machines, birds and animals, cities and jungles, laughter and weeping, prayer and cursing, birth and war, poetry and slander, meeting and parting, paper tearing and icebergs splitting, volcanoes erupting and spiders spinning, trees budding and stones tumbling, children whispering and crowds cheering, cliffs collapsing and sand sifting – and on the other, it sends forth its music through the furthest reaches of time and space, informing the blueness of sky and drip of stalactites, the movement of wind across prairies and blossoming of nebulae, the viscous nature of mud and celerity of cheetahs, the taste of wine and creak of leather, the fragility of snow and brightness of rubies, the surfacing of dolphins and touch of winter jasmine, the drifting of hours and pallor of linen, the fading of smoke and basking of a lizard, the strumming of

116

a guitar and scent of wild mint, the clarity of glass and coolness of dark passages, the cry of a toucan and flash of a car windscreen, the folding of cream and slap of waves, the brush of a hand on a cheek and sigh of a half-sleeping lover.

As he listens to the music of the shell, Kit suddenly realises that he is not simply a listener, but a part of it. All that he has been is drawn into the celestial spirals, and all that he will be emanates from them. His soul is an instrument in the eternal, unseen orchestra, and a voice in the unceasing choir. He feels insignificant, yet this is itself of no significance: it is an ecstatic, not a distressing, state of mind, for he sees that nothing matters but the whole and that nothing affords greater happiness than to be a part of it – like a thread in a tapestry, unnoticed yet indispensable to perfection, or a bee gathering sweetness for the hive. He laughs at the thought of of his perplexed, importunate, earthbound self.

'Every star has a voice,' says his great-grandfather; 'every raindrop and every prayer and every work of art, and all their voices are drawn, as in a whirlpool, into the heart of the shell. And at its centre they find the gift of harmony, cohere and are ushered out again. Now watch once more.'

So Kit lifts up his eyes, and sees the stars begin to fall.

My charter deal meant spending a week in Bodrum. I enjoyed discovering the pattern of Mum's new life – buying food from heaped stalls of exotic fruit and vegetables down on the quay, wandering dusty streets, getting to know other shopkeepers over small tumblers of sharp Turkish wine. We made little expeditions too, bumping our way over the plain past villages of whitewashed cottages with red-tiled roofs, each settlement clustered around an identical minaret. The soil was russet-coloured and so thickly littered with fragments of stone that it might have been a dust-sheet on the floor of a cosmic sculptor's studio; in places, however, it nurtured great sweeps of wild flowers. We encountered camels, men riding donkeys, old women labouring in waistcoats and baggy floral trousers. We stopped for picnics in groves where the drowsy hum of bees emanated from hives shaped like shoe-boxes. One day we searched the shoreline for a half-submerged city, and found only a herd of docile cows and some walls of questionable provenance; but this failure seemed unimportant as we stood on a sunny headland with poppies at our feet and strained our eyes towards a handful of distant islands.

Even on the most relaxed days though, memories of my father lay in wait for me like a spiky, poisonous fish below the calm of the bay. I dreaded having to go back to London and decide my next move.

'Come and see me again soon, darling,' Mum said as I prepared to board a midnight bus to Izmir for my return flight. I promised I would. We hugged each other close.

In the event, London was all right. The sun shone freshly, casting light like a bucket of water emptied across grimy pavements; the world seemed all the more vivid for my tiredness. I collapsed into bed and, after a few hours' sleep, set off down to the river to see my uncle.

'It's a bummer,' he said when I explained how Dad had anticipated my mission. 'But stay cool. We'll work something out.'

My mouth was dry as I said, 'Mum told me about what happened between you and Dad.'

He turned to watch one of those long vessels for collecting drift-wood as it passed downstream. He looked weary and rather old.

'I wish she hadn't,' he said. 'It's ancient history. No point in getting hassled about that now.'

'No point?' All the indignation I felt towards my father for what he'd done to Robbie, and my mother, and me, came together like a tidal wave building in unwatched reaches of the ocean. 'Robbie, my father may have changed the entire course of your life. You could be rich now; you could be a household name; you could have people queuing up to buy your paintings. Instead Dad earns a fortune, kow-towed to by everybody, and you're...'

'A failure?' He spoke quietly, with a half-smile on his face. 'If I may say so, that's a very Eighties attitude. Do you think I want to change places with your dad? OK, I could do with a radiator or two in the studio, but I get by. And if I said to you, hey, would you rather hang out with Sabrina or that Vicky person, you'd say Sabrina, right?'

I nodded.

'So your dad pulled a fast one on me. Maybe I'd have got to make *Heat* with Warhol. But for one thing I was never really into films, and for another that guy was seriously weird. I don't think we would have made a great team: in fact, given some of the things he was into, I'd probably have been dead before we finished shooting. So it could be that the cosmos was saying, "Keep out of this, man". It could be that your dad did me a favour.

'As for my paintings, some people would say that if they'd been good enough I would have become famous anyway. I don't buy that myself, because I know that the art world isn't so straightforward. But I do know that the work I did then means a lot less to me than what I'm doing now.'

'That's only natural,' I said. 'Every artist develops. It doesn't mean you can't be recognised for your early work *and* your later work.'

'True. But a lot of painters get so bogged down in that early stuff, or so strongly associated with it, that they can't escape into anything else. I sort of see myself as one of those game-show contestants where you have to choose between taking the prize you've got now or going on to try and win something bigger and better, only you might end up with nothing at all. It's like I said no to the dishwasher – or your dad said no for me – and now I'm trying for the deluxe caravan. If I'm going to be remembered, I want to be remembered for this.' He indicated half a dozen canvases stacked up around him.

'But even if we forget the about the consequences,' I protested, 'the fact remains that Dad betrayed you. Your best friend betrayed you, and you let him get away with it.'

'Friendship's a strange thing, isn't it? Of course it hurt me when I found out, but it didn't really surprise me. You have two people as close as we were, pursuing the same things, and in the end it's bound to go wrong. What's really weird is that it didn't happen sooner: if Tony hadn't got it together with your mum, we probably would have fallen out over some bird. So my attitude is, friendship is like love – just be grateful for what you had and don't let the end write off everything you had before. Blowing the whistle on your dad wouldn't have helped my career, and it would have been saying that all the good times we'd had together counted for nothing. As it is, I can look back on them and think, "That was groovy", whereas he can't look back on them without feeling guilty. And what's the future got for him when the bird in the swim-suit opens box number 13? More money, and Vicky – until she decides the time has come to cash her old man in. He's got the dishwasher; I've got my dreams. So don't feel sorry for me. I'm cool.'

I wasn't sure whether to shake him or recommend him for canonisation. 'But that's why this world is in such a mess. Because people like Dad and Vicky behave appallingly and nobody stops them.'

'Maybe it would be more of a mess if everyone was out for revenge.'

'Maybe.'

He gave me a look which made me feel very uncomfortable. 'About the cottage,' he said. 'You weren't thinking of, like, blackmail were you?'

'It had crossed my mind.'

'I want you to promise me that you'll forget it.'

'But – '

'Promise.'

I promised.

'What about Wednesday?' said my father. 'Come to the office at 11.30.'

He sounded cheerful, clearly believing I was about to accept his offer. I wasn't; nor, true to my word, was I going to blackmail him. What I hadn't promised Robbie, however, was to spare Dad the fact of my discovery; and I couldn't help hoping that shame might have the same effect as a threat.

'Really?' he said when I told him I'd just been to Turkey to see my mother; then added, as if discussing a vague acquaintance, 'What's she up to?'

I gave him a brief summary.

'That's good.'

'She told me about what happened between you and Robbie.'

'Oh?' His voice hardened. 'And what exactly did happen?'

I told him.

He leaned back, pressing his hands together as if in prayer. 'The trouble with hindsight,' he said at last, 'is that it oversimplifies so much. Artist drugs his partner, passes his work off as his own, and bingo! It seems pretty clear to you, doesn't it? Well, you may be interested to know that this moral leper you call your father doesn't quite see it like that.

'How much can one remember about something that happened 30 years ago? Not a great deal. A lot of it seems like an incident you've read about or watched on television rather than actually lived through. Besides which, the mind has a way of making its own adjustments: you start off by finding excuses for yourself and end up being completely convinced that you acted quite otherwise than you did. I don't believe that either I or Robbie would qualify as reliable witnesses in a court of law. Which of us has more to be ashamed of? Did I really double-cross him, or is he the one who's making excuses, because he's embarrassed by his failure?'

'Robbie's not making any excuses,' I said. 'He was careful not to tell me about this. And besides, he doesn't consider himself a failure.'

'But your mother does, doesn't she? So perhaps she's the one who's making excuses. You see how, the harder you look at it, the more complicated it becomes.

'Let's suppose that everything happened in the way your mother

120

describes. Would there necessarily have been anything as defined as a moment of moral choice? Imagine yourself sitting beside Warhol at the Factory while he leafs through the portfolios. You want him to be able to study them at leisure, so you try to act as if you're a million miles away. Perhaps he's pretty doped up as well and hasn't grasped which portfolio is yours or even that they're by two different people. He starts to go on about one set of pictures, and you nod your head, and by the time it dawns on you that he thinks they're your work rather than your friend's, it all seems too difficult to explain without making him appear a complete fool. Then when he starts talking about films, well, you know that's something you're interested in and Robbie isn't particularly, and suddenly this whole misunderstanding looks like providence...

'Of course I'm not saying that's what happened – it's simply the kind of thing that *could* have happened. But though I may not be sure of the facts, or of the rights and wrongs of it all, I can tell you one thing for certain: it isn't often that you get golden opportunities in life, and when you do, you've got to grab them with both hands. It's a jungle out there, and if you don't fight for yourself tooth and claw, you're going to end up as some big cat's plate of Meeow-Mix.'

It was a bravura performance. Indeed, if I hadn't known my father better I might have been taken in. As I had admitted to Robbie and Sabrina, things were seldom black-and-white. But I didn't believe for a moment that you could behave that way towards your best friend and not know for certain that it was despicable or remember every detail afterwards.

I wondered if Dad had always been like this. I found it hard to imagine how Robbie could have become friends with him if he had, or Mum have married him. Perhaps that silent pause in Warhol's Factory really had been a moment of choice. Perhaps the corridors of good and evil had stretched before him with terrifying clarity, and having chosen evil, he had run along it locking every door which might lead back to an honest view of himself.

I was tempted to rant and rave, but I was tired of these occasions disintegrating into shouting matches. Instead I said, 'How do I know I can trust you? How do I know you won't treat me the way you treated – might have treated – Robbie? You're the person most likely to make Meeow-Mix of me.'

He laughed, refusing to be bated. 'Don't worry about it. We'll have a contract drawn up, without any small print: your mother's half of the cottage at the price I paid for it, and the other half in return for your services. I'd hardly make you such a generous offer if I was planning to rip you off.'

'Why *are* you making me such a generous offer?'

'Because I think you're right for this campaign, and it happens to be a pretty important one, and I can't think of any other way of persuading you to do it. Besides which, you still happen to be my son.'

'That,' I said, 'is my bad luck, and if I was in a position to change it, I would. But since I'm not, I'll just say this: I think your behaviour towards all of us has been unspeakable, and I'd rather demolish the cottage with my bare hands than help with your lousy advertisements.'

And that, I imagined, was the end of that.

Ken. Stella still thought of him, occasionally dreamed of him. She couldn't understand why, but in her unguarded moments it was always the grinning snooker player who took shape first: the easy swagger with which he had approached the bar to chat her up; the feel of his bare arm through her blouse as he'd laid it nonchalantly across her shoulders; the flecks of beer froth on his trim moustache which she used to tease him about and lovingly wipe away. Coming to herself, she would focus on Kit – more relaxed now, but still silent, withdrawn – and the horror of that last visit would come crashing down on her like a dark breaker, leaving her breathless.

She didn't know who to blame, herself or fate: herself for falling for a man like Ken, or fate for taking him away. All she could be sure of was the painful, fearful chasm between what she had wanted and received. Oh, she had heard it over and over again, most recently from Michelle who'd moved in next door: 'First time I seen Dave, I'd have died laughing if you'd told me he was going to be my old man – that or slit my wrists. I'd been saving myself for Mel Gibson, see. Six months later we was going out, but I knew Mel would still come and get me. Now look at us – married five years next month, and never a cross word. Well, not often. The thing is, Stella, he's not just my old man, he's my best friend. If it had been Mel, I'd spend my whole life worrying about what he was up to with that Sigourney Weaver. Clyde's got a good heart; I'm not saying it'd be easy, mind, if you ever wanted to have kids and that, but you won't find a kinder man – and that's what counts in the end.'

Stella knew that what Michelle said was true, but part of her still rebelled against it. Some women got the man they longed for – why couldn't she be one of them? Yes, Clyde had all kinds of qualities that Ken lacked: he thought about things more and was more determined to do well out of life, not just drift along hoping to win the pools; he told her all sorts of things she'd never known about; he even cooked for her (though somehow that didn't seem quite right in a man); and, of course, he loved her. Yet still the devil inside her told her that by accepting him she would be settling for second best.

He worked that out soon enough. Sometimes, when she'd had a hard day or was particularly anxious about Kit, she couldn't make herself sound glad to hear from him over the telephone; once or twice she even snapped at him, then felt terrible about it, because he'd done nothing wrong – all he'd done was not be Ken. She knew when she'd hurt him, because he went all quiet, before deliberately changing the subject or ringing off with a promise to phone her again tomorrow. But he never snapped back or reproached her; and sometimes that only encouraged her devil and made it strike out more wildly. Increasingly though, the devil was cowed. She seemed to have been battering against a solid door and, as her strength failed her, began to realise that it was protecting rather than imprisoning her.

She kept what remained of Ken's things in the bottom of a chest of drawers. There was a Madness T-shirt, smelling a bit musty now, but she didn't have the heart to wash it; a programme from a Tottenham vs Everton match; a screwdriver with a handle which lit up; a studded belt which a mate had brought back from America, but which Ken had never worn; a mug with a Union Jack on it; a pair of Boots sunglasses; a can of shaving cream; a tube of hair gel; an out-of-date passport; a cassette of The Police's greatest hits in a scratched plastic case; a book of horoscopes.

Ken's interest in astrology had been an unexpected side to him – perhaps the only unexpected side. He had made a joke of it, but she noticed that the horoscopes were always the first thing he turned to in the newspaper. Though never really convinced, she had tried to share his interest, and after he had left her she had continued to follow the activities of Saturn and Mars. Might they be responsible for his departure? Would a sudden improvement in their aspects bring him back?

Now the paperback seemed like the dry shell of a dead insect; gradually other things in the drawer died too. Of what interest, she asked herself, could an old football programme be? The tube of gel felt faintly sticky, with a film of dust becoming cemented around some invisibly small puncture; the T-shirt, she came to admit, smelt quite unpleasant. She put them in a carrier bag, rolled it up and left it in a corner of the drawer.

The next day she went back, opened the bag and added other relics, coiling the belt neatly so that it fitted at the bottom. As casually as possible, she dropped it into the rubbish bin. Burning it would probably have given her more satisfaction, but it didn't seem a good idea on the eighth floor of a block of flats. She felt a little guilty about the perfectly good mug and the perfectly good screwdriver.

Waking in the early hours, she had to restrain herself from getting out of bed and hurrying to retrieve the once-precious hoard. Then the dustmen came and took it away.

She was glad to be going to Sebastian Terry's that day. She looked forward to her break and thumbing through those photographs. On arrival she put Kit down beside the radio and set to work on the kitchen floor, telling herself that she must ask Sebastian to get a new sponge for the mop. Next she dusted and Hoovered the bedroom. She had just got started on the bathroom when there was a buzz from the entry phone.

She ignored it at first. She'd got caught by Jehovah's Witnesses the previous week and didn't want to go through that again. But the caller persisted, and thinking it might be someone with an important parcel, she decided she'd better answer it.

'Hello,' came a voice so crackly that she'd could barely make it out. 'My name's Juliet Green. I'm Mr Terry's agent. I know he's not there at the moment, but he wanted me to collect some photographs, and he said you'd be able to let me in.'

'Oh, right,' said Stella. She didn't like the idea of a stranger barging in, particularly when Kit was there, but she didn't seem to have much choice. 'You'd better come up.'

'Which floor is it?'

'Second.' She pressed the button and looked quickly around to see if there was anything out of order. She'd better turn the radio off, just in case this agent person thought she was taking liberties. Then she put the door on the latch and went back to scouring.

She heard footsteps on the stairs becoming louder and the squeak of the front door. It needed some oil on the hinges: Sebastian wasn't very good about that sort of thing.

'Hello,' called a voice, and Stella started. It was a voice both very familiar and completely strange. She stepped out of the bathroom and stared in astonishment at the woman in the doorway.

'Hello, Vicks,' she said.

If possible, Vicky looked even more surprised than Stella. 'Hello, Sis,' she said at last. 'What are you doing here?'

'What's it look like?' Stella displayed her rubber gloves. 'I'm cleaning. What you doing here, more like? Since when you been anybody's agent? And since when you been called Juliet Green?'

Stella had never got on with Vicky at the best of times, and she was irritated by her hoity-toity new accent. There was no denying that she looked well-off though. What she was wearing wouldn't have been out of place in one of Mrs Elliot's wardrobes.

'It's a professional name. All agents have them. I've been in the business for a couple of years now.'

It was obvious she was lying. Stella wondered why.

'Vicky David always seemed a good enough name to me,' she said.

Vicky ignored her. 'You all right?' she asked.

'OK.'

'How's Mum?'

'Same as ever. Her chest's bad from all them fags. I don't see a lot of her.'

'Nor do I.'

'You should give her a call some time. She wonders what's happened to you.'

'I know. I must,' said Vicky. But Stella knew she had no intention of doing so.

'Close the door,' she said. 'I'll make us some coffee.'

'I can't stay. I've got a meeting. I'll just take these photographs and be off.'

'You've got time for some coffee.'

'All right then.'

It was strange for Stella to be in charge of the situation. When they were growing up it had always been Vicky, as the eldest, who gave orders. Something had rattled Vicky though, and it wasn't just the shock of running into her sister after so many years. (How many was it? Five? Six?) Stella was curious to find out what.

She led the way through the sitting-room into the kitchen. 'This is Kit,' she said, picking him up. 'Kit, this is your Auntie Vicks.'

'I didn't know you had a kid,' said Vicky. Her gaze flickered at the ring on her sister's left hand. 'Who's his dad?'

'No one you know,' said Stella quickly, setting Kit down and turning the radio back on. A dramatic aria sailed out of it.

'Ah, *Tosca*,' said Vicky, before realising that the remark was out of place. 'I saw it at Covent Garden a few weeks ago,' she added apologetically. 'Lovely opera.'

Stella raised her eyebrows. 'Spare us the airs and graces, Vicks. It's me, your sister, what you used to watch *Top of the Pops* with, all right?'

'Sorry,' said Vicky, looking embarrassed.

'You got any kids?'

'No, not yet.'

'Married?'

'Yes.'

'Nice, is he?'

'He looks after me.'

'That's good,' said Stella. 'I'll make the coffee.'

Vicky drifted back into the sitting-room. When Stella brought the coffee through, she was flicking through Sebastian's albums. 'Just trying to work out which one he wanted,' she said, with what seemed to Stella a guilty look.

'Coincidence, ain't it?' Stella put down the mugs. 'You being his agent and me his cleaning lady.'

Vicky looked anxious. 'I'd rather you didn't mention it to him, Stell,' she said. 'Don't get me wrong, it's not that I'm ashamed of where I come from or anything...'

'But?'

'It's just that – well, people like Sebastian tend to make assumptions about me, and if those assumptions turn out to be wrong, it's just very embarrassing for everybody.'

'I wonder what those assumptions are,' said Stella. 'I bet they think you grew up somewhere posher than Lambeth for a start.'

'Maybe. And if they do, I don't see that it's up to me to tell them otherwise. Or up to you for that matter.'

'You can't go through your whole life lying to people.'

'Lying? What's the truth? The truth is that I've got a great house and nice clothes and a new BMW, and you're still taking the bus and living in a lousy flat somewhere. I'm right, aren't I? That's all the truth I need. This is me, now: the past is nothing. The Vicky you used to know doesn't exist any more.'

'I still think people should be what they are.'

'No, Stell, you should be what you want to be, and don't let anyone stand in your way.' Vicky glared at her.

'What about your husband? Does he know?'

Vicky shook her head.

'Don't you think you ought to tell him?'

'What for? I fit into his world – that's why he married me. If I told him, he'd worry that I might embarrass him. He wouldn't thank me for making him feel uncomfortable.'

'I don't suppose he'd thank you for lying to him neither.'

'He's got plenty of secrets of his own, you can be sure of that. I don't go prying into them.'

'It don't sound like much of a marriage to me.'

'And how's your marriage, Stell? Husband got a job, has he? You just go out cleaning for a bit of pocket money, do you?'

Stella's confidence deserted her. Vicky had always been able to lock on to her weak spots; she always won in the end.

'I'm not married,' she said, staring at her cup of coffee and running her spoon across the surface like a sculler dipping an oar in a muddy estuary.

'There's something wrong with the kid, too, isn't there?'

'No.' Stella felt close to tears. 'There's nothing wrong with him.'

'Look,' said Vicky. Her tone, surprisingly, was conciliatory; for some reason she had decided not to press home her advantage. 'I know it's tough – that's why I had to get out and cut myself off. And even where I am now it's not exactly easy: wherever you go, you've got to screw people before they screw you. That's why I don't have any regrets about pulling the wool over their eyes. Sometimes I feel like standing up in the middle of a dinner party and saying, "Do you know what? I'm as common as muck!" just to see the look on their faces. And the thing is, they probably wouldn't believe me.'

She opened her handbag and took out a wad of £10 notes. 'This is for you, Stell, to make things a bit easier. I've got to be going now. I'll just take this portfolio with me – I think it's the one; yes, that's right. Say hello to Mum for me.'

Had it been any other album, she might have got away with it; but Stella recognised it instantly as the one with the strange abstracts in it – and on an impulse she reached forward and snatched it away.

'What the f--- are you doing?' asked Vicky furiously.

'How do I know you're really his agent?'

'What would I be doing here if I wasn't?'

Stella could think of no good answer; but her suspicions were not easily tamed. 'You've lied to everyone else,' she said. 'How do I know you're not lying to me?'

'So what do you think I'm trying to do with those photographs? Steal them?'

'Could be. I don't know. But I do know that that dosh is a bribe to keep my mouth shut.'

'God you're a suspicious cow!'

'You never was one for charity, Vicks.'

Vicky looked round as if appealing to the wallpaper for sympathy. 'Stell,' she said in a calmer voice, 'be reasonable. These photographs are needed for an important exhibition. It could be Sebastian's big break. If he finds that you've prevented them from being shown, he'll be furious. He might even sack you.'

'He didn't mention nothing to me about it. He would have rung or something. I can't go round handing his things to strangers. He might think I taken it myself. I'd get sacked for that more like.'

Vicky stood staring at her in silence, drumming her fingers against her thigh in the way she had when she was trying to make her mind up. 'OK,' she said at last. 'I don't want to get you into trouble. I won't tell Sebastian about this – I'll say I sent someone else who went to the wrong address. But you've got to promise me that you won't mention it either. He doesn't need to know anything more about me than he does already.'

'OK then.'

'Bye Stell.'

'Bye.'

Stella stood there with the portfolio grasped firmly in her arms until she heard the front door slam. Then she pulled her gloves on again and got back to work.

They were funny things, families, Stella thought to herself on the bus home. It was a shame you couldn't just put them together, like the sitcoms on TV: one glamorous, airheaded mother with endless strange crazes; one good-natured, exasperated father; a tone-deaf son who fancies himself as a rock star; a daughter always bringing home a new boyfriend... mix them together and there were lots of squabbles, but they all loved each other in the end. In life, though, it didn't seem to work like that – for her family, anyway. It was as if they were just a random selection of people who had been forced together, like strangers in an air-raid shelter during the Blitz; as soon as the all-clear had sounded, they had gone their separate ways. She didn't miss seeing her mother and sister: it always seemed to end in aggravation when she did. Dad, yes, though he'd been ill and sad and hen-pecked; and her grandparents – she had loved them.

128

She wanted better for Kit – but she knew she hadn't made a very good start of it. Her choice of a father for him had hardly been inspired. She thought of Mother Amelia with her big, happy family, and what she had said about Clyde; then she thought of Clyde and his endless, patient efforts to entertain Kit, and she laughed to herself. Clyde was made for fatherhood, just as she was made for motherhood – though of course that wasn't reason enough to marry him (and marriage, her instincts told her, was what he wanted). Could she love him enough? Perhaps.

Her mind went back to her sister. It was hard to believe that the girl in cheap mascara had turned into this rich, posh-sounding woman. But Vicky had always been ambitious, and she'd always known how to deal with men: even at school the bloke with the flashest bike seemed to be hers by right. There was no denying that she'd done well for herself. Stella tried to imagine what it would be like to own a brand-new BMW, but couldn't.

Vicky's appearance at Sebastian Terry's flat baffled her. Why had she lied about her name? Was she really a photographic agent? And if she wasn't, what – as she herself had said – was she doing there?

These questions gnawed at Stella over the following days. The only way to discover the truth was to tell Sebastian, which she had promised not to do. But then, she told herself, if Vicky had lied to her – and Stella was certain that she had – that promise was surely not binding. In the end she decided to leave it to providence: if Sebastian was there when she next went to clean his flat, she would ask him about his agent; if he wasn't, she would keep her mouth shut. As it turned out, he was.

'My agent?' he said, surprised. 'Jane Fletcher?' The name Juliet Green meant nothing to him. And so it all came out.

The discovery that her sister was Sebastian's stepmother – this unforeseen connection of two worlds – flabbergasted Stella. It meant that she and her employer were practically related – which, much as she liked him, was not something she felt very comfortable about. Could it be right for her to go around cleaning up after her step-nephew? She could hardly stop, needing the money as badly as she did, but she resented the fact that Vicky had put her in this position. Then she thought that maybe she had only herself to blame.

She wondered what kind of man Sebastian's father was: not very nice presumably, if he sent his wife round to steal his son's photographs. Clyde suggested in his mischievous way that she should go to her brother-in-law's office and introduce herself, but she knew that she would never have the courage. Besides, she couldn't see that she had any right to upset the apple cart. If anyone was going to do that, it should be Sebastian.

12.

I found it all too much to take in. Vicky had tried to steal my portfolio. The life story she had presented to me and everyone else was a
complete fabrication. On top of that, she was my cleaning lady's sister.

Even if I had seen her and Stella standing side by side, I would
never have guessed. Both were slightly above average height, but that
was as far as any physical resemblance went; Stella's demeanour was as
innocent as Vicky's was hard-bitten. As for the rest, Vicky had done an
impressive job of eradicating her South London accent and acquiring
extremely expensive tastes.

The attempted theft was just as amazing. I couldn't work out
whether they (I assumed Vicky had acted in collusion with my father)
had hoped to find another photographer who would be able to create
the same effect or simply intended to use the pictures without my permission, calculating that I would stop short of involving the family in a
law suit. This idea – that they would deliberately take advantage of my
good nature – made me particularly angry and resentful of the promise
I had given Robbie.

But then, when I'd made that promise we'd been talking about
Dad's past. It couldn't really apply to what I'd learnt about Vicky. What
should I do with this new bit of data? Use it to force her to backtrack
over the cottage? Simply lob it between her and my father and watch
what happened? The first option struck me as the more satisfying. Not
only would I get the cottage, but I would be able to laugh quietly at my
father – and enjoy Vicky's discomfort – for years to come.

After an initial sense of triumph, I began to feel ashamed of these
thoughts. I remembered what Robbie had said about forgiveness
and told myself that whatever action I took, it must not be motivated
by malice. Would it help Dad or make him happier to know that the
woman he had married was a liar? If I drove Vicky off, he might find
someone who would exert a more positive influence; but my mother
had done her best and had been made miserable. It seemed to me that

he and Vicky were well matched; neither should be inflicted on anyone else. Besides, as long as I had a hold over Vicky, I would be in a position to prevent her from doing too much damage.

On the other hand, there could surely be nothing wrong with using my new-found knowledge to secure what was mine. Vicky had persuaded my father to break his word and had tried to steal my photographs; now her false-heartedness was about to rebound on her. I didn't see myself as a blackmailer – more as an avenging angel.

'I suppose you must be feeling pretty pleased with yourself,' she said, driving her fork viciously into a spear of asparagus.

'I wouldn't say that. Pleased *for* myself, perhaps. I always like to see justice done – especially where I'm concerned.'

'I should have known better than to trust Stella to keep her mouth shut.'

'You should have known better than to try to steal my photographs. What I don't understand is that you knew there'd be someone in the flat, yet you didn't know that it would be your sister.'

'I had a man watching the place: he told me about the cleaning lady. Of course neither of us dreamed it would be someone I knew.'

'But even if the cleaning lady hadn't been Stella, she could have described you to me.'

'I was going to copy the pictures and put them back. There was no reason why you should have known anything about it.'

'Until the ads appeared.'

'And what would you have done then? Gone around telling everyone that your work had been pirated by your father?' She wiped a smear of hollandaise sauce from the corner of her mouth. 'Who would have believed you? Photographers are always coming up with "new" ideas that are remarkably similar to other people's. And even if they did believe you, why should they care?'

I was beginning to wish that I'd invited her somewhere less expensive for lunch than Botticelli's. The idea had been to show magnanimity in victory, but she was refusing to play the vanquished opponent in the way I hoped. Yes, she had agreed to my demands – that she would prevail on my father to sell me the cottage for the sum he had paid my mother; but I detected a spectacular absence of remorse.

'Whose idea was it?' I asked.

'Mine. Your father doesn't always have the drive he needs when it comes to realising goals. In my business we're more streamlined for industrial asset acquisition.'

She sounded like Becky Sharp teaching a graduate course in euphemism.

'I suppose I should be flattered that you consider me an industry. I prefer words like theft and plagiarism myself.'

She put down her fork and fixed me with eyes like granite. 'Don't get snotty with me, Sebastian. All right, you've got my number – but I've got yours too. Where would you be if you'd had the kind of upbringing I did? Do you think you'd have the luxury of taking arty photographs of mushrooms? It's your Dad's cash that's given you everything you've got, and now you're using blackmail to get more. Forget the moral high ground – you're standing on a bloody molehill.'

There were plenty of things I could have said in reply – that I'd rather have had a proper home than a posh education, that my father's fortunes stemmed from cheating my uncle, that I didn't consider morality a luxury. Instead, I changed the subject as calmly as I could and asked how she planned to persuade Dad to hand over the cottage.

'Don't worry about that,' she snapped. 'I'll deal with it.'

I had no doubt that she would.

I did have doubts, however, about whether I'd done the right thing. As I travelled home on the bus, sitting next to a man reading his tabloid newspaper with a magnifying glass, I couldn't help wondering how the small print of my life would stand up to scrutiny. I felt tainted by my encounter with Vicky, as if we were conspiring to defraud my father. Could I really have believed that I was doing him a favour by keeping her past a secret? Wasn't I living by the same dog-eat-dog principles as her?

I told myself to forget it. All that mattered was that I had got what I had struggled for: the cottage. I imagined the gate with its badly aligned bolt awaiting my attention; the stone floors biding their time in the afternoon sunlight; the water tank settled into absolute stillness. Nevertheless, the argument continued to spin through my head, like a jukebox disc on perpetual replay.

A week later Vicky phoned to say that my father had agreed to the change of plan. Then Robbie rang.

'Hey Silver Surfer,' he said. 'What's happening?'

'Nothing much,' I lied. What could I tell him? He would never believe that Vicky had experienced a Damascene conversion. He was bound to deduce that I had broken my promise to him.

We talked about this and that; but I had a sense that he too was holding something back. Finally he said, 'You know my Texan?'

'Yes.'

'He wants to buy every painting I've got in the studio.'

'You're joking.'

'No. He's going to have a special gallery built for them in Houston.'

I had a vision of red-necks in ten-gallon hats gawping at walls covered with my uncle's spaced-out fantasies.

'How many have you got?' I asked.

'About fifty – and he's talking about commissioning some murals too. This is big money. Which is partly what I wanted to talk to you about.'

'Why?'

'I thought it might solve your problem over the cottage. This will easily cover the dosh you need.'

'I've already got a mortgage,' I said. 'I can't afford to take on a loan as well.'

'We'll work something out. You can pay me back when the Texan gets into photographs. Or I'll just own half the place. Whatever.'

If only this had happened a week ago, I thought; it was too late now. Anyway, why should Dad receive all that money for the cottage – above all from the friend he had double-crossed?

'No,' I said. 'It's incredibly kind of you, Robbie, but I couldn't. I really couldn't.'

'I've got a surprise for you,' said Clyde.

'What is it?' asked Stella.

'Open it and see.'

He handed her a long white envelope. She unfolded the back flap, and took out two airline tickets. She stared at them in amazement.

'What...?'

'Look inside.'

Shaking her head and laughing, she opened the top ticket. 'London-Kingston,' she read. 'Where's that? There ain't no airport at Kingston. Shouldn't it say Heathrow?'

He laughed too. 'Not Kingston-on-Thames,' he said. 'Kingston, Jamaica. I'm taking you home for a holiday.'

'I don't believe it.'

'It's true. What more proof could you want than an airline ticket?'

'But how'd you get the money?'

'I've been saving. It wasn't that much – I've got a friend at church who works for a travel agent. He got me a special deal.'

'I don't believe it. All those beaches and things.'

He laughed again. 'Yes, all those beaches.'

She flung her arms around him. 'You're mad, you are.'

'We leave two weeks tomorrow. That all right with you?'

'Where we going to stay? We can't afford none of them hotels.'

'Don't worry. We'll stay with my cousins.'

'What about Kit? We can't go, love. I can't leave him.'

'Of course you can't. He's coming too. I reckon a little bit of sunshine is just what he needs.'

The stars fall not like shooting stars that scribble fire across the heavens but like fine drops of rain descending in blue light, cool and separate yet combining to spread a semi-opaque veil across the sky – like gauze shot through with silver threads – until the shell is entirely obscured. It is the blue of twilight passing over the world, soothing the earth after the heat of day; the blue in which men find their way home to rest and children spendthrift of their energy fall quiet at last and lovers wander with hands clasped and shoulders touching through cooling streets and fading parks and along deserted tow-paths where ducks and coots more heard than seen forage in black water. The gauze has the touch of soft rain that drifts across summer fields, reviving but not drenching, so that people lift their arms and laugh as they feel the vapours kiss their skin, just as it kissed leaves in the hedgerows and berries beneath them and stiff ears of corn and clods of dry earth. The music softens too, growing quieter, until it is a barely heard ripple, like the sound of a harp played in the lost depths of the sea.

This, Kit thinks, is peace such as he has never known. He feels as if he is being dissolved by the rain, as anxiety and memory and even thought fall away. He is becoming one of the drops, slipping downwards in gentle motion, tumbling with his brothers, sharing their brightness, fluidity; cascading through the firmament to be reabsorbed in the river of life. Around him he feels his own tears – those which he shed when he first reached the bridge; but instead of tears of sorrow they have been transformed into tears of joy.

As he wonders at this, he becomes aware of a bright light refracting through liquid stars. At first it is merely a glint, like that of a silver coin glimpsed through long grass. While he watches however, it grows in intensity, banishing twilight and overwhelming all he can see with such a pure whiteness that, but for the veil of tears, he feels he would be blinded or consumed. But a cloudburst of stars interprets the light, dancing before it, alchemising it into a spectrum so vivid that it is as if colours were being created for the first time, struck from their transparency with the freshness of a child's thought: red like the essence of sunrise over a painted desert; orange like newly grated carrot glistening with olive oil; yellow like a crowd of buttercups still cradling dew; green like an ungrazed meadow after a last melting of snow; blue like summer sea wrapped in summer sky; indigo like a length of silk raised dripping from a vat of dye; violet like its own flowers glowing in a hollow at dusk... a rainbow spanning the heavens like the broadest arch of an ethereal cathedral fashioned from perfect crystal.

'Behold,' says the old man beside him, 'the promise of life: the seven colours of the rainbow, the seven ages of man, each with its interplay of divine light and mortal tears. The first age you yourself have known – the blaze of celestial light in which a soul enters the world, like a piece of newly forged metalwork before it is plunged into the blacksmith's pool. Then comes childhood, with joy of discovery and thrill of knowledge and easy giving of affection – but drawing on too of man's worst traits, selfishness and cruelty. Thirdly, adolescence and its extremes of happiness and pain, with first love and vivid dreaming set against self-doubt and insecurity, in a hall of mirrors where everything is multiplied and distorted but a single image of beauty can stay with you while life endures. Next adulthood, where the labyrinth resolves itself into a handful of corridors from which to choose your way, and independence is bought with responsibility. Marriage follows, like the trellis on which these roses climb – a fence of love that offers guidance and support; yet the neglected blossom turns away its head, and storm-damage leaves the structure leaning in the wind. Then parenthood, which drags you forever outside yourself on tides of love and anxiety. Finally, in the violet evening, you gather your life's rewards – loneliness or wide affection, serenity or regret – until death brings the last reward of all.'

Now, before their eyes, the rainbow divides itself, flowing into the seven rivers that flow into the river of life.

'Why have I been shown this?' asks Kit.

'Because,' says the old man, 'you have a choice. You may, if you wish, remain here; or you may return to the world from which you have come. You have been shown the rainbow so that you know what lies ahead of you on earth – though you will not remember it if you decide to go back there.'

'I don't understand,' says Kit. 'Who would possibly choose that discordant world in preference to the music that surrounds us here?'

'You forget that the earth contributes to this music; that although those who sing there are deaf to it, except in snatches, their voices are as important as if they were here. To despise the world is to despise the most beautiful part of creation.'

'But it is still imperfect,' protests Kit; 'and when one has known perfection, it is surely impossible to be content with anything else.'

'There is virtue, however, in contrast.'

Kit shakes his head. 'The perfection I have found here is full of variety. There is nothing static about it. It is a river, ever changing, ever the same. There is no need to look for contrast.'

His great-grandfather smiles. 'Imagine a journey to a foreign land. You may not like it as well as your own, but it offers different things. Above all, whether you enjoy it or not, it leaves you wiser, helps you to develop; and souls develop just as people do. There is no pleasure for a teacher in giving a pupil the answer to a problem – the pleasure lies in seeing that pupil follow steps he has been taught and find the answer for himself.

'But to return to our journey: although it may appear to be an end in itself, it is the sense of being away that gives it richness, and coming home that validates it. Equally, it is only through absence that you can truly value your home.

'So you may, if you choose, remain here; or you may return there, and grow, and gain in wisdom, and bring greater joy to your creator and joy to those who love you there.'

Kit stares at the turbulence of the waters below him. There seems to be a danger in them that he had not sensed before. He is afraid of drowning – of disappearing for ever beneath that wild, white surface. 'How can I be certain,' he asks, 'of coming home a second time?'

'You have seen the rainbow,' says the old man gently. 'You can be certain.'

Kit sits on the bridge for a long while, watching the waves and eddies move in ecstatic, graceful time to the music around them. 'In a moment,' he thinks, 'I will find the courage.' Then at last he stands and embraces the old man, and turns to dive into the whorls of foam.

It was a grey, humid day when I drove up to take possession of the cottage. A haze hung over the Cotswolds like damp muslin stretched over a bowl, and even in shirt sleeves I felt sticky as I left the main road and swung slowly through twisting country lanes. It was odd to think that on arrival there would be nothing to prevent me from turning on the boiler and running a hot bath.

I had arranged for someone from the village to keep an eye on the garden, but it had been some time since his last visit. An ungoverned rose bush tugged at my clothes as I pushed through the gate, its thick flowers interspersed with dead heads which had dried and flattened like tiny starfish. A watering-can stood half-full of rusty rainwater.

Inside the cottage was cool and silent. Mr Czernowsky's usurping possessions had gone: the dresser stood bare of plates, windows denuded of curtains. A layer of dust had built up on the side-table where his ranks of photographs had once been. I moved through the rooms, letting my eyes run over ceilings and walls and corners, feeling the dry, splintered roughness of beams and lintels, establishing my presence and ownership. I felt like an aborigine wandering through the Australian continent, naming things into existence.

I stared at the fireplace in the drawing-room, with its pale landscape of ashes and a half-burnt log lying where it had fallen on Mr Czernowsky's last evening. I opened a heavy wardrobe, empty except for a bundle of clothes-hangers. I turned a brass tap and felt it choke into life. The sun came out for the first time that day, and I watched shadows fall where they had always been accustomed to fall.

After exploring the upper rooms, I went downstairs and sat on a chair beside the cold Aga. Under my feet the broad flagstones were as pockmarked as I remembered from days when my toy cars had hurtled across them. But it did not feel as if the house belonged to me any more than it had to Mr Czernowsky. We two were merely passers-through, inhabiting a space which had been – and would be – occupied by others. The cottage was more than any of us, and it had no favourites.

So this was what I had struggled for – this silence, this neutrality. I had opened the door expecting my past happiness to greet me like an overenthusiastic dog. But it wasn't there. It had gone. History had slipped out the back.

The wretchedness of that thought cannot be described. So much for the photographer who believed he could capture the moment for ever; so much for the man who – in his arrogance – had made the most instantaneous and elusive of life-forms, the light-shy mushroom, his prey. The whole centre of my life had been called into question.

'Here you are,' said a voice. 'This is what you wanted, isn't it? Well, now you've got it. So what are you going to do with it?'

I looked around at the table and cupboards and chairs. They

seemed to echo the question. 'We're waiting. We're here to serve you, as we served your predecessor. No, we don't remember you. Memory is not one of our duties. Just tell us what you want to happen.'

I couldn't bear their indifference. I wanted to shout, 'Forget the future – give me back the past!' But I knew that my words would simply be absorbed by the shadows. I leapt up, knocking over my chair, and hurried out into the lane.

There was no one in sight. I strode towards the church and turned right into a field bisected by a public footpath. Under the trees a huddle of cows stared at me with minimal curiosity.

The hedgerows were white with fretty chervil and the red earth was dry underfoot. I followed the path uphill, crossing a ramshackle stile and skirting a field of cabbages. I wondered how long it was since I had last come this way. I guessed twenty years.

As I reached the next gate, a black and white dog appeared on the far side and began to bark. Had I met it in the middle of the field, I would probably have walked straight on; but since I had the protection of the gate, I stood there until the dog's owner arrived to take control of her animal.

'He doesn't bite,' she said, as if surprised by my timidity. 'He's just nervous, that's all.'

Humiliated, I stumped on in a worse frame of mind. The hill was much steeper now, and before long my shirt was sticking to my back. On top of that, my shoes were inadequate for the rough, stony ground. I could feel the ruts through their thin soles.

My mind meanwhile ran over the same questions again and again. Was it a rule of life that what we most longed for lost its allure once attained? Had I spoiled everything by breaking my word to my uncle? Or had my whole enterprise been misguided from the start?

It seemed to me now that it was the very fleetingness of the past which made it so attractive. Wasn't it like the Sixties songs that I loved? I could buy them on compilation albums, capture them from the air-waves at the touch of a recording button; but that didn't begin to compare with the excitement I had known as a child, before I could afford records, when I'd huddled beneath the bedclothes with my mother's transistor radio pressed against my ear and finally heard a DJ somewhere out in the North Sea announcing the song I longed to hear: 'And now a classic from a few years ago, Bob Lind with *Elusive Butterfly*...' Only that thrill, which could never be regained, could never be devalued.

Pausing to look around, I realised I had missed my way. The path seemed clear enough, but the gate to which it led was half the length of the field from where I had expected. Either my memory had played me false, or in my depressed state I had failed to take sufficient note of where I was going. I changed course, heading towards a straggling line of trees.

When I reached them, I knew exactly where I was. The ground fell away sharply into what was almost a gully, providing – in winter – a perfect toboggan run. I had been there hundreds of times in my childhood, first with a tin tray on which I had slithered awkwardly down the lower slopes, later with a proper wooden sled – a Christmas present from my mother and father. How many times I had hauled it up the hill, clutching the rope with wet mittens, frozen breath clouding the air and condensing in tiny droplets on my balaclava helmet! There had been nothing to beat the thrill of stretching out on the wooden slats and launching myself downwards, gathering speed till the trees became a blur and nothing was real except the bumping of half-airborne runners over frozen earth.

At that moment of surprised recognition, my dark mood lifted and I found myself filled with joy. I felt like a tennis player who hits a winning shot, his heart as taut as the strings across his racquet; or a polevaulter sailing upwards to straddle the challenging bar. It was as if, in approaching the familiar spot from an unaccustomed direction, I was seeing it for the first time – just as, following my guide through the foreign side-streets of Bodrum, I had come round the corner and caught sight of my mother transformed by happiness. As I looked down the valley, I realised that everything might be all right after all – that what I had thought a false end might prove a new beginning, and that in seeking to recapture the past I had perhaps finally managed to escape it.

I must have stood there motionless for ten or fifteen minutes, spinning out the sensation. Then, leaning back against a tree, I began to ruminate on the consequences of what had passed. I had fallen out with my father, probably irreversibly, yet that was far less important than having re-established contact with my mother; and the cottage, despite my disappointment, might still be a home. I knew that I had made grave errors, but none seemed inescapable in this wide world of possibilities.

The future was waiting like the pristine slope stretched out on a snowy morning, calling to a young tobogganist to launch himself if he dared. Laughing out loud, I pushed myself away from the tree and started to run downhill, my heart growing fuller as the valley rushed up to meet me.

In the warm waters of the Caribbean, Kit reaches towards bright shoals of fish as they arc vividly past. They are as strange and colourful as those he saw in the aquarium at Kew, but they move more joyfully, with the freedom of the ocean. He splashes, laughing, trying to grasp them. Clyde smiles and holds him firmly in his strong brown arms.

Behind them, on the beach – a white scimitar of sand – Stella watches the fronds of palm leaves high above moving in the breeze like feathers of an exotic, languid bird. The clear blue of the sea, washed with brightness by a sun that magics every wave into an intricate, delicate, momentary diadem, makes her want to cry at its beauty. The hardships of London have no relevance now; she has been reborn. She will ask Clyde if they can stay here for ever.

There is no one else on the beach apart from two fishermen resting by their boat. Stella found them hard to understand when Clyde spoke to them earlier, but she enjoyed watching him joke with them. Now they break into song, their voices borne towards her on the breeze. *'Many rivers to cross,'* they sing, *'but I can't find my way over...'*

Out in the shallows, Kit hears them and is briefly distracted from the submarine world whirling before his eyes. 'The rivers of heaven,' he thinks. 'The rivers of heaven...'

But he cannot visualise the rivers of heaven. Their memory has all but vanished from his mind, like smoke from a candle burning in bright sunlight, detectable only by its sparse, wavering shadow.

Made in the USA
Las Vegas, NV
11 January 2021